Rosieta Rosalini

by

Cecil Horn

**Grosvenor House
Publishing Limited**

The right of Cecil Horn to be identified as the author of this
work has been asserted by her in accordance with Section 78
of the Copyright, Designs and Patents Act 1988

The book cover picture is copyright to Cecil Horn

This book is published by
Grosvenor House Publishing Ltd
28-30 High Street, Guildford, Surrey, GU1 3EL.
www.grosvenorhousepublishing.co.uk

A CIP record for this book
is available from the British Library

ISBN 978-1-78148-381-7

Chapter One

Rosieta Rosalini

It is April, the sun is shining, birds are singing. It is quite idyllic, but it is shopping day. Something that does not inspire me. Arriving at the supermarket car park I am a little more pleased as there are not many here, but at the trolley park I become a little less happy.

There is a lady trying to disentangle her trolley from the rest. Her lips are moving but I can't hear what she is saying. I think it is not at all complimentary to the trolley. With one great tug it comes free and her brolly falls to the ground, and also knocks mine down. They now lie together.

Seeing the rather frustrated, even annoyed look on my face, the lady burst out laughing, attracting a number of glances from other shoppers, and when she went to pick her umbrella up, it was entangled with mine and she burst out laughing again. The situation now was bordering on the ridiculous, and I just had to join her in her laughter, and it was even attracting chuckles from other shoppers. That was just the start of a very unusual day; I would even say extraordinary day.

The lady has left the trolley that she had fought so hard to get, and is now dancing and singing to the strains of singing in the rain. Her dancing is beautiful, almost professional. She is almost floating on air. She has a lovely slim figure and the dancing seems quite effortless. As I make my way into the store, she gently takes hold of me and gracefully moves around me, throws her brolly up in the air, catches it, and with the other hand reaches up to see if it was still raining; unlikely as we were in the store.

Still going through the air, she decides that this time I should be moving around her, and she begins to do this, but now there is a gasp from the little crowd. The lady has collapsed and is now clinging onto me very tightly, and she does not move. I call frantically, "Get a chair please, quickly" and two chairs soon arrive. I lower her gently into one, and I take the other one. She has not relaxed her grip. Her knuckles are white on her hands. There are calls from her little crowd, "Is she alright? Is she alright?" Now a sigh from her little gathering, for she has opened her eyes. The people that had been watching her were, I think, afraid of what was going through my mind. Would she dance no more? Had all her happiness meant her death?

She raised her head as she turned to the little group and said, "Thank you, everyone. I am so sorry if I have worried you all. I have been told many times that I must not do this, and still I do it." Still holding tight onto me she continued, "I hope it might help you to understand if I tell you that for eighteen years I was a professional ballet dancer, and I did, and still do, love to dance. When I feel happy I am gliding across the floor with my 'Rudolph Neres', who today happens to be this nice gentleman here. I don't know his name as we have only just met at the trolley park, but I hope he will tell me", and a slight cheek goes up. "It was this nice gentleman who brought it all on. He made me laugh, and as I laughed I was happy; and happiness to me is to imagine I am at the London Coliseum, or Covent Garden Theatres, gliding across the stage with those lovely dresses and beautiful music. I thank you all so much."

What is happening here? The manager has arrived, and does not appear too happy. Before he can destroy the lady's happiness I stand up, after making sure the lady was okay. "This lady was quite overcome by her memories of her career in ballet, and just had to dance, which we have all enjoyed immensely. If you upset her, you upset us, your customers." "Thank you", he said, and paused. "Jim", I said, "Thank you Jim. I certainly was not going to do that. You see, I knew just what happened here. My secretary had told me. I just had to be sure that the lady was alright". He took the lady's hand and asked her, "Are you alright now?" "Yes", she said. "I am fine". Now he said, "I must insist that you both come to my office. It will not take long. "Oh no", said the little group that had gathered. "Nothing like that", he said. "I am not going to have a moan. I admire them both. They are going to enjoy with me a glass of champagne. They are by no means young people, and they have put a great deal into their show this morning and in doing so they have shown me that life really is what you make it, and I thank them". He took hold of the lady's hand, and I took the lady's other arm, and we very gently made our way to the office.

Now he takes the lady's hands and gently lowers her into one of his very push arm chairs, while looking into her eyes with a smile. He seems as captivated as the rest of us. Now don't think I was annoyed about the disruption this morning, because in the little crowd was an old friend of mine. A reporter on the local paper, and so I think we will all make the front page tomorrow. The secretary has poured the champagne and we each have a glass, and the manager raises his glass and begins. "I wish you both many more happy years and I hope it is together. I think you have found something. Hold onto it, and each other. Now I know your name, Jim, but we don't know the name of the lovely lady". Very quietly she said, "My name is Rosieta Rosalini". She did not say any more but she had a smile from ear to ear. Rosieta could see in our faces the look of amazement, and to have her name recognised by us all just increased that smile.

"Now", said the manager, "I must hand you over to my secretary, Stephanie, who will take you home. When you get home, I want you to write out the list of all the things that you would have bought today, and give it to Stephanie, and all the things that you have listed will be delivered to you tomorrow, absolutely free of charge with my best wishes." Now we both have beaming grins. "While it gives me great pleasure to do this, I have to tell you that the call that I have just answered was from the local paper. It looks as if we will all get a reward from your show, and so I thank you! Now I must leave you as I have to prepare for some guys from London. Goodbye, and again my very best wishes to you both". Stephanie takes us through the store, and as we go we get a few cheers from some of the shoppers. Now she takes us to her car and tells us what she is going to do. "I am going around the car park and I would like you to show me your cars. Give me the keys, which I will leave in my office, for whoever you choose to collect them. Is that alright?"

I have suggested to Rosieta that perhaps she might like to come to my house for a coffee and a chat about this extraordinary day and she has agreed and said that she would like that very much.

We are here now and I go ahead and unlock the door. Stephanie takes Rosieta by the hand, very carefully, and hands her to me. "Now I need that list", she said, as she turned to go back to the car.

When she returns, she has the remains of the champagne and, placing it on the table she turned to us and said, "If I were you I would add a few luxuries to celebrate". We laughed, and did. "Have you a camera, Jim?" "Yes", he said. "Well I would like a couple of pictures. Would you mind?" We could hardly refuse. "Is that alright, Rosieta?" I said. "Yes, I would like that very much. This day has been like a page from Grimm's Fairy Tales to me, and the photos would always remind me of it all".

Stephanie arranged us on the settee together, looking like a couple of teenagers, with smiles from ear to ear, and in truth that is how they felt.

"Now", said Stephanie, "If I arrange the camera carefully and squeeze in between you I could have a picture with you and I would like that. Would you mind?" "We would like that, Stephanie. Please do".

Now she shows us on screen what she has taken, and we were so glad that she had suggested it. Now this day will last forever. "Well, Jim and Rosieta, if I don't get back very soon, he will wonder where I have been, and so I had better make a move".

Rosieta and I stood up and we each gave Stephanie a big hug, which was returned with a big kiss for both of us. I think Stephanie would have liked to have stayed a little longer, but I think she knew the manager a little better than we.

We waved as she went and sat back on the settee with another glass of champagne, and we began going back over the day, both so happy the day had been so extraordinary, how it all came about, my reaction to her trolley wrestling, and her reaction to my expression. "I was a little annoyed at being help up", she just had to laugh, and I joined her. What a crazy day indeed. But this happy day was born and just became happier.

Because we were so happy and content sitting there cheek to cheek, I know it might sound a little crazy, but this feeling soon had us fast asleep. We were of course in our seventies, and at that age a nap come very easily.

Rosieta wakes first. "Goodness me! Look at the time. It is almost one o'clock. What about lunch?" Her rather startled expression woke Jim. "What's the problem, Rosieta? What about lunch?"

Jim's favourite expression was "It will be alright", and he turned to Rosieta, put his arm around her, and very calmly said, "We are eating out". "You never said", Rosieta replied, and Jim calmly again said, "That's because I did not know", and even that brought on a chuckle.

When Chris and Ruth brought the cars back I had asked them to leave mine on the road as I might be needing it. Today is a day when you take it as it comes.

"Come along, Rosieta. Your golden coach awaits" and we make it to the car. Chris and Ruth are in the garden and introductions are made. It looks as though we are going to get on fine.

"Now I am going to take this young lady out to lunch. Come on Rosieta, your golden coach awaits!"

With a few more waves we are on our way and I make my way to a lovely village pub at Westwell called 'The Wheel'. It is a pub that the modernisers have not yet torn the heart out of. That is not to say that it lacks warmth and expression; it is there in abundance.

On entering, we are met by a charming young lady, and I ask for a meal in a secluded area if she could please. She grinned, and said, "Not newlyweds?" "No", I said, "But if we told you of all that has happened today you would not believe us, and I am determined to preserve it for as long as I can. Now the young lady had a lovely smile, and found us a table in a little alcove. "Thank you", we said, and her smile said all the very best to you both. She brought our meal and we thoroughly enjoyed it. I am sure it was cooked on the premises and not 'bought in'. We were not anxious to leave, and time had flown by, when the young lady approached us. "Oh dear", said Rosieta, "Are we holding you up?" "No", she said, "Not at all, but you looked so serenely happy that I wondered if you would tell me a little of this extraordinary day that you have mentioned. "Just a little?" Well we did and she could hardly believe it, and neither can we.

We made our way to the door and pay our bill, and she had a strange sort of smile. It seemed to say "How I would like to read the back page of this story", or perhaps she wondered how many pages there would be. But neither Rosieta nor I will think of that.

On arriving at number 33, Rosie was pleased to see her car up the drive, and we came in and sat back on the settee, still this wonderful day brought its pleasures, but I fear I must raise the nasty face of reality. We must come back to Earth some time. I don't want to do it, but I think I must.

"Rosie?" "Yes, Jim, what's on your mind?" she said with a chuckle, which brought the same from Jim. Not that he said something a little more serious.

You have two sons, and I have a son, and daughter. They must be put in the picture. This brought a long pause. "Yes", said Rosie. "You are quite right. I have been trying very hard not to think of anything that could cast a cloud over this wonderful day. Could we not leave it until tomorrow?" "I don't think so, Rosie. There are too many implications. I think a couple of hours this evening would be necessary to put our families' minds at ease, and if, as I think, they could possibly destroy that which we have found, we could resume this wonderful like that we have found, and feel much more at ease. Now how do you feel about it, Rosie? I would like to phone my son and daughter, Rosie, and invite them here this evening, so that we can all talk this over. Now what do you think, Rosie? Would you be prepared to do the same? There is nothing that cannot be overcome. We are both of sound mind. It is we that are calling the shots. We are really just doing what we believe to be right, and I am sure they will see it in the same way, and a happy evening will be the crowning glory of our day. Well, that is as I see it, Rosie, but I must know if you wholeheartedly agree or not; we are not going to do anything unless we both are of the same mind." "I know you are right, Jim, and to be really honest, it is good to hear a really decisive man beside me, and when the first real problem occurs, he is ready to act. You go ahead, Jim, and I will call my two sons. What do you think about seven o'clock?" "Yes, I think that will be fine", he said, but deep down he was a little worried.

Jim had painted a nice amicable picture, but they were both very much on edge; what Jim and Rosie were planning to do did have serious implications, especially for Richard, her youngest son, who lived with his mother. Jim and Rosie of course could see only the rose-tinted picture of a lovely last few years together, but only if they had the blessing of all the members of both their families. If they could not have this then it was a non-starter; they were old-fashioned still in their beliefs that the family came before themselves.

The first one has arrived and as we expected it is Richard. Rosie was quickly at the door to welcome him. She brought him into the room, and taking Jim's arm, said "This is Jim". Richard and Jim shake hands and do their best to put each other at ease. "Until this morning I did not know Jim", she said, "But now I would like to stay with him, but only with the blessing of you, and John. Don't say anything now, Richard, as I hope we are all going to enjoy a pleasant evening.

"One day Richard", said Jim, "We will tell you the whole extraordinary story. It is quite incredible. A whirl-wind of a day that has brought Rosieta and I very great happiness, but of course implications for our families; that is why we hoped you would all be here this evening." We talked about some of the things that had happened today, until John and his wife, Sandra, arrived. Again, Rosieta was soon at the door. John gave his mother a kiss and helped Sandra into the room. Sandra is expecting their baby, which cannot be far away. She was quite pleased to sit down, and I introduced myself and said, "I expect you are getting a little impatient". "I am", she said, with a sigh.

Now I went back to John. We shook hands, looked on rather nervously by Rosieta. "Thank you for coming, John. We do realise it was rather short notice, but

Rosieta and I felt that her family and mine should know what we have in mind. It has been an extraordinary day, and when we tell you the whole story you will see just how extraordinary. But let us have a pleasant evening first". Ron, Jim's son has now arrived with his daughter, Pam. I know Pam will be fine, but Ron, who has spent his life in finance, is always on the look-out for a dodgy deal, and will not hesitate to remark on what he sees. My turn now. I go to the door; a hug for Pam and a handshake for Ron, and I take them in to meet Rosieta's family. "This is my son, Ron, and my daughter, Pam. This lovely lady is Rosieta, and her two sons, Richard and John". She gave Pam a kiss, and one for Ron, which seemed to take a little longer. "Well, as much as I enjoyed that, Rosieta" Ron said, "I do think I should go back to the car and get my lady, Jean", and this definitely broke the ice.

He brought Jean in, and I did my best to apologise with a big hug and a kiss, and she just smiled as she always did. "Now if you are happy for me to do so, I would like to assume the position of chairman", and they gave me a soft clapping with a chuckle. "I have told you of a little that has happened today, and we would not blame you if you have a picture of two seventy plussers behaving like two teenagers, but to see us as we really are, to really understand how we feel, you would have to know all that has happened during this fairytale of a day. But I do not think we could do justice to this wonderful day in the time we have this evening".

"I will, however, tell you how it all began – arrived at the supermarket a very reluctant shopper; not something that I enjoy, and at the trolley park, things looked like getting a little less of a joy. I took hold of my trolley but hesitated as there was a lady in the other line, wrestling with her trolley, obviously saying some very uncomplimentary things to it, and with one almighty tug it was free. In the process, her umbrella falls to the ground, and knocks mine down as well. Now she looks up at me; she sees this rather frustrated look on my face, even a little angry, and bursts out laughing. This, of course, also did not impress me. She now goes to pick up her umbrella and it is entangled with mine, and she laughs again. The situation was now becoming a little on the crazy side and now I too just had to laugh. Then to my amazement, she left the trolley that she had fought so hard to get and began to dance to the strains of 'Singing in the Rain'. I later learnt who this beautiful dancer was. It was that famous dancer of a few years ago, Rosieta Rosalini".

"You may all see later why these seventy-plussers think they are teenagers. We just ask you not to judge us too harshly, and now we must know your thoughts on what we propose doing. This day has been so absolutely wonderful that we think that together the autumn of our lives could be just as wonderful, if we stayed together. We know what problems this could bring, that is why we have asked you all here this evening. To do what we plan would in time affect you all. That is why we must have your blessing, given quite unreservedly, or it cannot take place. I would like to say here and now that if we do live this autumn of our lives together, then any decision of us both will be discussed most carefully by us all, as we are, now, in this room. Both our families are of the utmost importance. Now because Richard will be most affected, we would like him to begin; the house will be a quiet as mine since Marjorie died, but he is still a young man, and I think he will not have too much of a problem. I do hope he can see it this way. Thank you, Richard."

"You are right: Richard will be adaptable. I shall do my utmost to help you both, because looking at you I see what I have lost. I remember my teenage days when everything is so important, leading up to my married life. What could possibly get in the way? But something did, and we parted, and I came back to my mum. I shall pour no cold water on this dream, but wish you all the very best in this, the autumn of your lives. But I want you to both to remember that, like John, Pam and Ron, I shall not be far away. Do please call us if you are in trouble. We all softly clapped, knowing how difficult it must have been for Richard.

John now stands and begins his little speech. "Seeing you sitting there looking so happy is a joy to see, and it seems you are the reason, Jim", and as John looks at this mother, her smile increases. "You, mother, and Jim, will have talked this lovely plan over, and Jim will, I think will have spotted a few problems, but we will not think of those this evening, but just wish you both some wonderful years ahead, al the very best for the future from myself and Sandra, and like Richard, do please give us a call if you have a problem. We will be quickly with you". A little soft applause from John and now Ron must wish them well. After such lovely words from Richard and John, it is going to be a little difficult for Ron. He knows he should point out some obvious problems with this future that Jim and Rosieta plan; but equally he knows he cannot do it. He is not going to be the one to pour cold water on this dream. This fairytale Rosieta and Jim plan may only last for days, months, a year or two. How could he deny them the great happiness that they both see ahead? They see no clouds, the sky is blue, as blue as those lovely eyes of Rosieta, and Ron knows that he must wish them well. "Well, Rosieta, and my 'dear father', it is my pleasure now to say a few words, and I know I could not put it any more lovingly than the words spoken by Richard and John. You will by now have a good idea of the reaction of us all to that which you are planning. Because Richard and John have already said it all, all I have to do is just rubber-stamp it 'application accepted'. But that I could never do, because I want you to know that I too feel that what you have found you must hold onto. You must give it all you have got, be those young teenagers, live life to the full with all you have left, and remember my motto: 'It will be alright'. Again, as with Richard and John, Jean and I are never far from a phone. We will always be ready, and most willing to be with you. Call us please".

Now with all the loving terms spoken by the family, what was there left for Pam to say? She had the most difficult position, but because she was a woman, she would have a slightly different viewpoint. "Thanks you, Rosieta and Dad. It is indeed a pleasure to be here this evening, and to witness this wonderful dream unfolding. Countless numbers of older people in the autumn of their lives would envy you, and you have everything to make it work. You even have a back-up team of three young men and me, who would be with you in an instant if you have trouble. This being so, you must go for it. Remember Ron's motto, 'It will be alright', and those other well-remembered words, 'I may not pass this way again". I think that is all I have to say. Please do it,

Jim and Rosieta, and I shall live it with you. All the very best to you both.

Rosieta and I stand up and get a little cheek and a clap and I sit Rosieta down. "Now", I said, "There is only one of us who has not spoken, and I think we would all like to hear from her", and I get a few "here heres". "But Jim! You have put it so well I can't improve on that, and come on Rosieta. Just a few words." "Alright, Jim. If it will please you that much". Rosieta went over the trolley park. The grumpy old guy who stood beside her, the laughter it brought on. Dancing with Jim as her 'Rudolph Nureyev', the very happy situation just made her dance, with those lovely dresses and beautiful music, and the sheer joy when she was asked her name, when she replied Rosieta Rosalini. This lady was a famous ballerina! You could almost hear the little group marvel at the thought. This was that lovely ballerina, still dancing.

"This was just the start of my fantastic day with Jim. I would take much longer than the time that we have to tell you all that has happened in the hours of this day, but I hope what I have said in my own words, with no prompting, will help confirm in your own minds that this is what Jim and I really want. The wonderful words you have all spoken were what we were hoping to hear from you all, but if you found you could not have given us your blessings; then we would have abandoned our dream. Neither of us would have risked hurting our families in any way.

That is not to say that Jim and I could do that easily. What we have here is indeed a fairy-tale, and we would have for evermore been looking over our shoulders for our fairy Godmother, with that golden coach to take us back to that dream. Thank you all so very much". I sit Rosieta down very carefully and round off the evening. "Thank you all for coming, especially at such very short notice. You have been very kind; you have made us feel that our dream is indeed liveable. Our world is at the moment upside down, but we are going to go for it. We may lose our way as we wander through this beautiful autumnal haze, but we will not call you unless we really can't find our way out. Just one more thing. Nothing will be even considered by Rosieta and I, which affects any of us, without you first being invited here to discuss it; all of you. Thank you again". Rosieta stands up and our guests prepare to leave. Rosieta looks at me and smiles; she has the look of a very happy lady.

Everybody gets a hug and a kiss, and the evening ends. Rosieta was so pleased that it went so well. Everyone seemed in a happy mood. Now as 'seventy plus', our life can begin, and with one great big hug and a kiss, we both fall back on the settee, happily exhausted. "Well, Rosie. I am feeling absolutely tired out. How about a nice cup of chocolate and off to bed?" "Goodness me! I have no night clothes, Jim." Suddenly we were getting down to the basics of what we planned. Having no night clothes hit Rosie like a ton of bricks; it was obviously very important to her, and so I set about finding a compromise. "I have some pyjamas that I never wear. I find them too restrictive. Would they do? I always sleep in my birthday suit." There was no comment from Rosie, and so Jim went to the kitchen to make their drinks. As we were drinking it, I glanced out of the corner of my eye, and that rather startled look had largely disappeared. Rosie looked a little more relaxed, and she turned to me and quietly said, "Jim, would you mind if I too slept in my birthday suit?" He smiled. It was quite clear that here was a lady who would do nothing that was the slightest bit outrageous. "Rosie", he said, "you are still a lovely lady: slim, with a lovely figure, nice pink cheeks, and hair that many ladies would love to have. What a question to ask of any man."

"Any man, me included, be he nine to ninety, would be so happy to lie beside you. Just because you have lost the bloom of your youth does not mean that we are unattractive to the right partner, and for me you are that person. I would love to be with you. There is one other thing though Rosie, where would you like to sleep? You could have my room with the single bed, or we could share the double bed." This really made her think. There was a gap in the conversation, and then very softly she said, "I would like to be with you, Jim." With a big hug everything was settled.

Again, my highly-planned life has changed. Rosie has grabbed the bathroom, but this was good as by the time I came out of the bathroom, Rosie was under the sheets and her modesty was protected. As I undressed, Rosie said, "Jim, I never asked you which side of the bed you preferred." "Oh, I am not fussy. I am happy either side." As he got down to the last item of his clothing it was quite obvious that she was far more relaxed, as she said, "Not bad. Not bad." And with a laugh I climbed into bed. We snuggled up to each other and talked of all that happened. It was still hard to believe, a wonderful day indeed. But I would not have been a man if this lovely lady who lay beside me, 'seventy plus' she may have been, but to me of similar age she was beautiful, and as we looked at each other, words were not important.

I woke first in the morning and lay looking at her, wondering if I should pinch myself to see if it was all real. When Rosie's eyes opened, and they quickly developed into an impish grin which brought about a grin on Jim which sort of said, "I have climbed Everest", they suddenly both seemed very pleased with themselves. Hardly a word was said, but those grins remained. Rosie slid out of bed and headed for the bathroom, still keeping that impish grin on Jim, and as she closed the door, her head appeared with the question, "Jim, what is the oldest age in this country that a woman has become pregnant?!" Jim could see what she was up to. She was trying to scare him a little and so he said, "Eighty five, I believe" and all went quiet. As Rosieta came back from the bathroom, Jim took a gentle but firm hold of her, looked her straight in the eyes, and said, "Rosie, I don't know the age of the oldest pregnancy in this country", and they both had a good chuckle. They had both won, and another lovely day had dawned.

Chapter Two

Memories

"Jim", Rosie called. "I must go to my house today to collect some dresses. I have been invited by my school. The letter has just arrived." "A little late for an old girls' reunion. What's it all about?" said Jim. "This is not an old girls' reunion. I have been invited to give a talk on my life in ballet dancing to the sixth form, and it would give me great pleasure if I could start one of these girls on the fantastic voyage of life that I have had, and am still having with you, Jim. The school is where it all began and I cannot forget all that I have loved about my career being largely due to that school."

When we arrived at Rosie's house, I was quite impressed. It was a little bigger than mine, and it was carefully tended by a lady, and it set me thinking. Rosie was quite happy with me at the moment but she had been used to a far grander life, although perhaps not lately. I do hope that being back in her old home will not make her want to return, but whatever she wanted she will have. I can deny her nothing; she has given me a new lease of life. We went up to the bedroom. Again, it was beautifully furnished. She opened the wardrobe and it was fairyland again. In the wardrobe there were beautiful gowns of red, green, sky blue, made of a silky material that shone in the morning sunlight, and I could already see her in them. She held up several against her and asked me my opinion. "Which do you think suits me the best, Jim?" "Rosie" I said, "On you they all look marvellous." "You are just on big flatterer, Jim. You say the nicest things. But today please Jim, I would like your honest opinion. Which of these dresses would be best for the school?" "Go through them again and I will say just what comes into my mind. I will tell you in which one you look the most beautiful.

"Well" said Jim. "It was difficult. They are all very beautiful dresses, but with your blue eyes and lovely blonde hair, and that smile. "Oh come on, Jim. Which one?" "The blue one, Rosie" he said, as he realised he had slightly overdone it. Every woman loves a little flattering, but Jim did rather overdo it, and this time he knew it. "Thank you, Jim. Now I will slip into the other room and try it on. I hope it still first. I have not worn it for a year or two. I very much hope it does." When she came back, she had tousled her hair, done a little makeup job, and there she stood in that lovely sky blue dress. When I think of that term 'heavenly issue", she was it, and with that smile she was all ready to go to the ball, after the ballet.

Again that awful feeling went through my mind. How could I hold onto her? Would my humdrum life be too dull for her, and would I lose her? "Well, you wanted my honest opinion, Rosie and here it is. Are you ready? You look absolutely beautiful. You could go anywhere." And his words drained away until Rosie could not hear him, not like Jim. "What is wrong, Jim? Tell me what is wrong." Jim did not want to say what he was thinking, but Rosie insisted, "Tell me, Jim. What is wrong? This is not like you. Have a problem? Tell me." "Alright, Rosie. I will. I did not want to but I cannot allow you to be worried about me. It is not physical. It is emotional. Looking at you in that lovely dress, you looked beautiful, fit for a king, and an awful thought went through my mind. How can I possibly keep this beautiful lady in my world? It bears no resemblance to the world she has known, and could so easily know again. What will I do it I lose her?" To my utter amazement, she flung her arms around me. "The dress, Rosie. The dress." I said. "To blazes with the dress. It is you that I want, and she planted a great big kiss on my lips, and we both had grins from ear to ear. "You have made me smile, Rosie. What a gal you are! But I think we should finish what we came here to do." And still with that grin she said, "Yes, Jim!"

Rosie closes the wardrobe door and packs the dresses in their boxes, which had probably been used many times, and as we head for the door, I turn and have a glance at Rosie, and as I thought, she was having a long, lingering look at her old bedroom, but she had reassured me a little earlier, and I felt a little easier.

With her dresses, she brought her makeup case and jewellery, and today we see the finished article. She is determined to be seen as that great ballet dancer, when we arrive at the school at two thirty.

Rosie is a little nervous. It is a few years since she stood before an audience, but now she is putting on the dress, and whatever else she thinks will impress. Fortunately for me, I am not involved here. As I am all dressed and ready to go, I am sure that very few will notice me, and so I sit and wait for the queen of

Sheba, and here she is. "Rosie, are you sure you will not outshine the leading lady?" "Oh shut up, Jim! How do I look? Can you see anything out of place?" "Not a thing, Rosie. You look lovely. You shall go to the ball." Jim was doing all he could to stop her worrying about her performance, as it had been a few years since her last, but he need not have had any concerns. It all came back to her.

"Time to go, Rosie", and he gently took her by the hand, and with a big smile he sat her in the car. "Now have a quick think, Rosieta. Have you got everything? Are you sure you have not forgotten something?" "No, James. There is nothing."

"Now if I am to be Rosieta, Jim, you are going to be James", she said with a chuckle. "Yes, ma'am", said Jim. They arrived at the school and parked the car, a little further along by the main door, were the reception committee, who were coming to meet us. I now have Rosieta out of the car and she goes to the head mistress for the introductions. "This lady, ladies and gentlemen, who I am sure you all recognise, is that famous ballerina, Rosieta Rosalini, of not so long ago, whose performances I for one seldom missed.

She then runs through the rest of the committee, paying particular attention to her head girl, Francisca, of whom she has great hopes. I am now alongside Rosieta, and she introduces me as her very good friend, James. The rest of the people now go to the hall, while Rosieta and I are taken to the headmistress's study, where she outlines just what she would like. "Rosieta, I consider this a great honour, and I thank you now, and welcome you and James here to our school. I have been most impressed over the years when I have seen performances, performed by a girl from this school, and I have tried very hard with a group of my present girls to emulate your great achievements. My girls are going to perform the first act of Swan Lake. That beautiful ballet that I am sure you are very, very familiar with. I know it cannot be quite up to your excellent standards, but I do hope that you can enjoy it. And if after the performance you could say a few inspiring words, it would mean so much. The girls have all tried so hard, and they would be so impressed, coming from the lady who has done so much for ballet".

"In particular, Rosieta, I would like you if you could say a few very inspirational words to my head girl, Francisa. It is she that I hope will be my next Rosieta Rosalini. Thank you again, and now we will take our seats in the front row at the ballet. The head mistress was a very happy woman. This was doing her career no harm at all.

Here we are with all the dignitaries. On stage there is the piano, violin, cello and the harp; all to be played by the students and here come the fairies. Rosieta, I am sure, was looking for dancing skills, but I just wished I was fifty years younger. They were indeed not just students, but beautiful young ladies, and they floated on in lovely pale green dresses, followed by Francisca in a beautiful white dress. To me they danced superbly. I am sure Rosieta, with me, was back in fairy land.

I had a quick glance at Rosieta and she was almost out of her seat, and the head mistress had taken her hand. A look of extreme eagerness on Rosieta, and a lovely smile on the head mistress, Julie. I think Julie could not have been more pleased.

These young ladies were not professional dancers, but the performance they had produced was, even to me, fantastic. The music, the atmosphere, the dresses, I am sure, must have had Rosieta back at Covent Garden or The Coliseum Theatres. Julie the head must have realised this, and held Rosieta's hand tightly.

End of act one Swan Lake. I could almost hear Rosieta shouting for me, but it is back to the real world and Rosieta now has to do her part. Julie takes Rosieta carefully up onto the stage, where she looks out at the audience. She has not been in this position for a number of years and would have to admit to being slightly nervous, but here we go. "Ladies and Gentleman. It gives me great pleasure to be here today, to hear the beautiful music and see those lovely dresses, and to see such excellent dancing by these young ladies in those dresses. It has been many years since I stood where these young ladies stand today, but I have to say that the performance given by them today was every bit as good as mine would have been, when I was at this school, doing what they have done today. This being so, I have no hesitation in saying that I believe that should any of them wish to continue in ballet, they will have no problems. I wish them well."

"As for Francisca, her performance was also excellent, and I would be a little disappointed if the dancing ability she has shown today was not used to the full in the future. The school I think could have another Margo Fonteyn." Then she turned to the girls who had danced so well. "What I have said girls, I meant your performance was excellent. Your elegant movement, your slight smile, general deportment, all were there in your dancing, and you could all be fine ballerinas, and

I thank you all. You have taken me back where it all began; it has been a wonderful life. Many thanks also to Julie, the head mistress. She could not have known I am sure, what immense pleasure it would give me to be part of this beautiful performance of Swan Lake, and to be amongst all the people here today, who so obviously have the school very much at heart. Thank you all so very much."

They stood and applauded her as Julie took her gently across the stage to her study. Having seated us comfortably, Julie asked for tea and cakes to be sent in, she then turned to Rosieta with a beaming smile, and endeavoured to thank her enough, which she found a little difficult. Julie the head mistress was literally over the moon. The visit of Rosieta had been a resounding success. Not only had Rosieta without doubt inspired her girls with her after-show speech, but the head mistress could see her prestige boosted considerably

The refreshments have arrived, Julie thanks the young lady and proceeds to hand round the cakes and pour the tea, still with that look of somebody who has just won the lottery. After outlining her plans for the school, and especially the ballet class, with a little more general chat it was time to go, and while the head, Julie, had gained much prestige Rosieta had regained that pride which she knew after every performance in years gone by, and both ladies were very happy.

Taking Rosieta's arm as if she was made of priceless china, we moved gently towards our car. Francisca opens the door, Rosieta is gently helped into her seat, and with suitable hugs, kisses and waves, were are on our way. To be honest, I was a little relieved to be on our way. I did really enjoy the ballet performance of

Swan Lake, but I am not one for formalities. I was, however, so very pleased to see Rosieta so happy, back in the world she had so loved. Nothing I could have suggested could have lived up to the sheer joy that she had experienced today. As we drove home I turned to offer my congratulations, and I was a little taken aback, for there were tears in her eyes, and she had her hanky in her hand. It was no hard to understand why and I stopped the car. I wrap my arms around her and she finishes the job; she burst into tears and it is obvious what is wrong. She is quite overcome by all that has happened today.

She has achieved so much fame in her life, but she is deep down a very unassuming lady, and while she has enjoyed the day immensely, it is now, after the show, that it has hit her, and I feel quite helpless. What could I say? Fortunately she let me off the hook. "Sorry, Jim" she said. "The day has been wonderful and I have loved it. While I was part of it I felt I could go on and on, but now I know that I am not as young as those lovely girls, and I have a different set of rules to abide by, but my love of ballet will always be with me."

"I would not want you any other way, Rosieta. Up there on the stage you were still that famous ballerina, almost directing the show. Mentally it is still all there, but we move a little more slowly now. That is not to say that you cannot continue to be that famous ballerina Rosieta Rosalini. The only one I was so proud to be with on this marvellous day, and those tears were only to be expected after a day like today that has meant so much to you. Now shall we head for home, Rosie, or shall we go to the ball? With that dress you would fit the bill beautifully." "Let's go home, Jim."

Chapter Three

A Difficult Situation

On reaching home the first job was to put that dress back into the wardrobe. I think she secretly hoped it would be needed again, and that it would always fit her. We had a leisurely evening and an early night. Rosieta was so tired. It is days like this that make us realised that we are not as young as we were. Today it is a lovely morning and Rosieta thinks she would like to spend the day in the garden with me. I think that would be good for her. I have always found that while gardening can be physically tiring, it can be mentally refreshing, and after yesterday, I think she might need a little relaxing.

We are getting along quite well with our different tasks when Rosie calls, "Jim, I have been thinking." "That's nice", said Jim. "What about?" "If we took that old cherry out we could get half a dozen roses in there. What do you think?" "What I think, Rosie is that a nice cup of coffee would be nice." "Yes, Jim, and I will make it." And while Rosie is doing it, Jim can think. The last thing he wants to do is to upset her. He loves his new life.

Jim sits down in the sunhouse. The sun is lovely and he must think of a suitable reply to Rosie's question without making her unhappy. He felt he was skating on very thin ice. Rosie brings the coffee, places it on the table and snuggles up to Jim. This was great. Now Jim wraps his arms around her and pulls her close, so that her cheek is against his, and in the position she cannot look him in the eyes. He is so concerned about her reaction to what he has to say. "It is fifty years now, Rosie, since I came here. It was so nice to have a newly built house, but the garden was just a field with great tufts of grass, and next day was like today, and I just lay in that grass. My neighbour thought I was lazy, but I was thinking how I would lay it out. She rushed into it and I think she was sorry afterwards. As things grew, I was quite pleased and took my photos which hang on my wall. Now when I see them I remember how it was. After has taken its toll, and it no longer has that cared-for appearance, but I still see it as it was and would like to keep it that way."

"When you suggested working in the garden, I was so pleased, and it did feel so good, with both of us working together. The birds were singing, fruit trees and flowers in bloom; all was well with the world. I was so pleased to have you with me." There he stopped, and waited in a silence that was full of expectation. It did not last long. They had a sip of their coffee and Rosie began to speak. "Jim", she said. "I think I have been a little bit thoughtless." That hit Jim rather hard and he released her completely and looked at her with loving eyes. "No!" she said. "Don't say anything, Jim. Let me speak my piece. I have seen those pictures on the wall, the pictures of the garden the way it has been. It has been a beautiful garden and I have tried to imagine what the gardener was thinking as he took those photos of his creation. He would have been full of pride as he looked at such a beautiful scene and I am sure there was no better garden anywhere near. It is not the garden it was, but we all grow older, and look a little more untidy. But I would like to work with you, Jim, to bring it back to the beautiful garden it has been, without any major alterations, keeping it like those pictures on the wall." And he gets a big smacker and a hug with her usual beaming smile. "Thank you, Rosie. I shall love working with you in the garden, and thanks for letting me down so very lightly without one harsh word. I sometimes wonder if you have any. Now shall we continue where we left off before coffee break?" And it was so good for Jim to have a partner again.

Chapter Four

Grandma Rosie

There will be no harsh words today. John's wife, Sandra, has gone into hospital to have her baby. Rosieta will be thinking of the day when John was born and that wonderful feeling when the baby is placed in Mum's arms. Of course there is a little work to be done before that can happen, but most mums think it is worth it. All went well and Sandra has a little boy. She is now a proud mum, and of course Rosieta is now a Grandma; a lovely sight. Two very happy ladies. The little boy's name will be Paul John Rosalini; quite a mouthful. He is already making himself a real blue-eyed boy with his Grandma Rosieta. We are quite often here now. I do hope Rosie does not overdo it, after all there is another grandma, Sandra's mum. At the moment, Rosie is very welcome as Sandra needs a babysitter while she goes to art classes etcetera, and this suits Rosie very nicely. But I don't think that she has given much thought to the other grandma. Rosie, I think, is in danger of monopolising the situation, but I am standing well back!

Of course while Grandma's love it, Grandads are not so keen. Jim likes it when the youngster is about two years old, and starts to make things a little difficult for mum and dad, and raises a laugh for granddad, quietly, that is! All this interest in young Paul is presenting Jim with another problem. He would like to go for a holiday, but how could be interest Rosie when she feels so needed and loved by that little charmer, Paul. I know Rosie would have a fantastic holiday and although she would be enjoying it so, there would in back of her mind be that wonderful homecoming when she held that little charmer again. I had, of course, not looked at it through the eyes of Grandma Rosie. She would see the other Grandma, Hazel, quickly taking over. After all, Hazel being Sandra's mother could expect the most important roles. It was fortunate for Rosie that Hazel was a rather quiet lady, who preferred a quiet life.

Again, Jim had that nagging thought of lack of appeal, when he thought of that loving relationship that Rosie had with young Paul, and Sandra's need of her babysitter. How could he get her to drop everything and fly away with him? It would only be for two weeks, and he would find a way, and this wonderful new life must be lived to the full while they both had the energy to do it. The lines of that tune, 'September Song', kept going through his mind. "And I haven't got time for the waiting game", he would go, and he would have Rosie with him. That is all on hold today. I must go and visit an old friend of mine, Fred. His wife has told me of his fall, and his injuries. She is rather concerned about his attitude. He is allowing it to get him down, and of course being about my age, that is not too difficult to imagine. We worked in neighbouring workshops and so I should be able to think of a few situations that will raise a laugh, although with cracked ribs he would not want to get too hysterical!

When I arrive at Fred's house, his wife, Jean, opens the door, and there is a look of relief on her face. She is a lovely lady, but she has not been able to shake Fred out of it, and it's dragging herself down as well. It was good to see him again. Years have gone by and many things have happened, so much to remember and talk about, and Jean, his wife, is happy to leave us to it and catch up on her work. I was happy to help Fred and Jean, but suddenly I realised just how many years had gone by, and of course how much older I was. But this is where one must say I am as old as I feel, and I am ready for Everest. Time has flown by. Jean, Fred and I have had a good chat over a cup of coffee, and now I must go, and I could see how it brought a little happiness to Jean and Fred. When one gets older, visitors grow less. A firm handshake from Fred and Jean takes me to the door. She gives me a good hug, and a peck, and I know she is a little more relieved, and I am so pleased for them both. Jim's route home took him by a travel shop and in the window there was a feature on Canada, and thinking there might be more in the brochures inside, Jim went in and took two.

When he arrived home, Rosie asked about Fred and what were the booklets for. Jim explained what he had seen in the window and how it had stirred his imagination, as his geographical interest in that country had always been quite strong, and he said that he thought there might be more in the brochures. "And was there?" said Rosie. "No" Jim said, "But they might be interesting." Jim went into the greenhouse for an hour or two, and when he came back into the house, he could see that the brochures were not where he had left them; not just tidied, but obviously looked at. Now that was interesting. "Jim" Rosie says. "I have had a quick glance at those brochures." "Oh yes?" said Jim. "Anything of interest?" "Yes" she said. "They mentioned Montreal and Toronto, and I remembered where in those cities I had danced. It all seemed so clear. The theatres were large and beautiful, and the Canadian people almost made me think that I was Canadian. Do you think that we are too told to go back there one day, Jim? What a chance, what a bit of luck. All the thought he had put into it, and now it drops into his lap. It is now or never. He will not get a better chance. Here we go. "Rosie" he said. "I do not like that world old. I much prefer older. Yes, we are indeed older, quite a lot older than when you danced there, but we can still walk, and you can still dance. And so there is no reason why we could not go, of that is what we want."

Jim knew this would bring Rosie's next question, "Do we both want to go, Jim? Or is it just me with my wanderlust? I did get quite carried away." "I would love to go to Canada, Rosie. We are most definitely not too old. Canada is a country that has always stirred my imagination. Its geography is so extremely varied, Rockies, coniferous forests, glaciers and so much more. "You sound even more enthusiastic than me, Jim". "Oh that is just because geology and geography are my pet subjects. But you know, Rosie, if we are both sure, we should do it soon, while we are both young, and she laughed. That evening, she talked of nothing else, on and on. Jim had started something, but now he felt that he had just got to turn her off and he said calmly, "Do you think Paul would miss you?" It was like a sudden braking in the car; silence, not a sound. Jim loved to chat with Rosie, but is had been almost continuous. He just had to have a rest.

Next morning after breakfast, Rosie calmly said, "I'm going to see Sandra." "Oh yes?" says Jim. "Anything you would like me to do?" "No" said Rosie, and off she goes. It was quite obvious where she was going. Rosieta arrived at Sandra's and the door was opened. "How nice to see you. Come in, my dear. My mother's here, so we can all have a nice chat" and there was Sandra's mum, Hazel, with young Paul on her lap, both looking very happy. The scene was quite different to what Rosie had expected, but it all went along very well. The chatting was very pleasant, and young Paul looked so happy that there would be no problem there, and after a pleasant afternoon she prepared to make her exit. "It has been very nice. I have enjoyed it and to find hazel here as well, that also was great, as we do not often meet do we?" And she gets a nice smile from Hazel.

"Just one more thing, ladies. Jim and I are going to take a holiday." With a sort of excited surprise they both said "Where?" "We are going to Canada!" "Oh, how lovely" they said. "When?" "Well, we have only just decided, and so it will be in a few weeks yet". "What made you decide on Canada, Rosieta?" "Well I have danced in Montreal, and Toronto, and I would just love to go back. But this time I will have time to see the lovely country, and enjoy the trip on that famous train, 'The Rocky Mountaineer'" "Oh Rosie, how wonderful. But what about Jim?" "Well it was he that started it all. He left some brochures lying on the settee, and I had a look through them. I am not so sure that they were not left there to get my thinking. Jim loves geology and geography, and in a country like Canada, he says both his subjects will be there in spectacular abundance, and he will have me." "It sounds quite idyllic, and Hazel and I both really envy you." With hugs and kisses from the ladies, and the shape of two red lips on the top of young Paul's head, Rosieta is on her way, so pleased with the way it had all gone. It had been so pleasant, and Hazel and Sandra really were so happy for both Jim and Rosieta. It was quite obvious they were not just being polite.

Jim sees Rosie go by the window and prepares himself for whatever was about to happen! There she stands; the picture of triumphant happiness! Stand by! Prepare for action! "Ring the tour company, Jim, we are on our way!" "Whatever happened, Rosie? Let's have it, I can't stand the suspense!" "Okay, Jim, but could you do one little thing first? Could you make a cup of tea while I go to the bathroom? Yahoo!" Tea is made. Jim is standing by for the big announcement. "It went marvellously, Jim" and Rosie went through the happenings of the afternoon. "Young Paul seemed so happy with Hazel, and both Sandra and Hazel seemed really happy to see me, but what really surprised me was their reaction when I said we were going on holiday. They both excitedly said together, "Where?" and when I said Canada, with Montreal, Toronto, and the Rocky Mountaineer, with all those other places like Niagara Falls, and coming back across Canada on the 'Transcontinental' to our aircraft to fly home, well, they both said, "Rosieta, we are both so envious of you and hope you enjoy every minute."

"They were so envious that I was a little embarrassed, so with everything dropping into place, is that Canadian enthusiasm still there, Jim?" "Mine is, Rosie, what about you?" "I just can't wait, Jim. I feel that our whole experience is about to begin again, but I will feel happier when we are both on that aircraft; then I will know it is really happening." John, Rosieta's son, phoned in the evening, not to wish her bon voyage, but to reassure himself that this was not a step too far; that her teenage enthusiasm was not going to put her in a difficult position, far away where he or the family could not help her. It was obvious that he would never talk her out of it. Her excitement was boiling over, and he accepted the situation. She just had to go, but he asked Rosie and Jim to allow him to arrange it all for them, which they gratefully accepted.

We had the same offer from Richard, Pam and Paul, which we thanked them for, but explained that John had already asked if he could do it, and that we had accepted. We are both very excited, and to have all of the arrangements like passports, currency, timing, and many other things taken on by the family make it feel even better, They seem very happy to do it, but I am sure in the back of their minds they are asking each other, "Do you think they will be alright?" Ron, of course, will say what he ways says, "It will be alright."

Chapter Five

Canada Here We Come

The whole family have been as good as their word, and the day has arrived. All are here to wish us bon voyage, although it is by air. There are a few watery eyes, not through sadness, but sheer joy, and we feel it so very much ourselves. The holiday has a courtesy car included in the package tour to take us to Heathrow airport, and it has arrived. The driver looks a nice guy and he has loaded the luggage into the boot. With some great hugs and kisses to and from the family, almost like we would not be coming back, we get into the car, and with much waving we pull away. But as happy as we were, we still had room for a few butterflies in the stomach; after all we have felt we could climb Everest. Now we were going to find out just what we could do! No trouble getting to Heathrow. The driver's sat nav took us right to the doors. Just one problem – we are half an hour too early, and we can't find the tour rep.

The tour rep has now arrived at the scheduled time. A very pleasant lady and she soon passes us through luggage check and security, and now we being the long walk to gate 46. Nobody seems to be waiting at gate 46, and I make a few enquiries, and I am informed that the

Vancouver flight will now be going from gate 45. I hope this is not a bad omen.

On the aircraft now, a little more tightly packed than I would have liked, but I guess that is how they keep the price down. I don't think I would like to pay 'Business Class' at two thousand pounds plus. Rosieta has flown many times, but this is only my second flight, and the first one was only ten minutes and that was just me and the Canadian pilot in a wartime fighter aircraft. He said, "Now I am going to give you air training corps boys. A ten minute trip, but if the Gerry's arrive, you will be down pronto. I think whatever happens on this flight, it could never thrill me the way that Canadian pilot did. I think the grin on his face said it all, but it was something that any boy would have given his whole year's sweet ration for.

The Canadians were great fighters, but I think they were not too keen on the "yes sir, no sir" stuff, and I had a distinct feeling that our flights were very much 'off the records'. Great guys.

This aircraft is so big compared to those little wartime fighters, but here we go. Slowly, we taxi to the runway. The engines roar, speed increases, and the aircraft almost stands on its tail as it heads to its cruising height. Having reached that height, we are now told what this and that are, and how we escape in the unlikely event that it would be necessary!

I don't think that I am going to be too happy with what the stewardess says will be a nine hour flight; perhaps Rosie has a few suggestions. Rosie is just so happy to be on her way. To her, a nine hour flight is a small price to pay, and she takes my hand. I think she thinks I am a little worried about flying, but today I am fine.

I had thought for many years what would be my reaction to flying. Would I at the last moment say no, and refuse? But it was just like getting on a bus, and sitting here with Rosie is great, but I think nine hours will bore me to tears.

Well it was not so bad. The food was a bit grim, but we are just touching down at Vancouver. Not bad. We left Heathrow at 1815 hours, and arrived here at 1835 hours, Canadian time. Rosie and I are both so excited.

We are taken to our hotel; a very large building, and because of its size, we have to use the lifts. I hate them, but Rosie leads the way. Better I guess than using the stairs to the tenth floor.

Our room seems enormous, nearly as big as my house. Everything seems so big, even the bed must, I think, be a king sixe, but I am ready for it. I just couldn't seem to sleep on the plane. But I think because we were both tired, we did have a good night's sleep, and now for day!

•

Chapter Six

Vancouver

We tour Vancouver in the morning; the tower and market place etcetera. It was the market place that gave me my first surprise; while looking through my pocket for another ten cents, a lady standing beside me put down a dollar coin and said, "Give the Englishman what he wants, please." I thanked her very much and realised again what a wonderful people the Canadians are.

In the afternoon, we visit the Capilano Suspension bridge, over this rather deep gorge, and when we reach the other side, after swaying about somewhat, there is a sign saying 'Congratulations. You have made it. A little scary but well worth it'. Now we are off to the Grosu Mountain ride. The cable car reaches 3700 feet in eight minutes. Here at the top, we look out over coniferous forests, not a building in sight, giving us the feeling that a man has never been here. There is none of that blue haze that hangs over our country, and the air is like perfume; marvellous.

I was quite surprised to find at the top there is some ice and frost, but some of the trees are a little more golden. Rosie is please that she has a light coat with her.

But I think it would take something quite devastation to remove that smile of satisfaction. She can stop and soak it all up. When she was on tour, she could not.

A very early start today. 6.30 and we are just about to board the rocky mountaineer. Rosie's excitement grows. This is what she so wanted to do, and the weather is great. The sun has just risen and is now just touching the tips of the Rockies, and here we go. Our destination is Kamloops, 247 miles of shining lakes, White Water Rivers and, of course, the Rockies. Another large hotel and more elevators, but I leave those to Rosie.

Another early start today, 310 miles to Banff but what miles they were. We have climbed considerably now, and down below on the railway is a freight train. It has 143 trucks, with three engines. Because the track is carved through the Rockies, the train must stop for a rock fall from above. The Rockies are crumbling a little. We have arrived at Banff, 4500 feet above sea level. Our room tonight will be one of the 180 rooms in this hotel called 'The Inns of Banff'; same excellent service, same smiling faces.

A change of transport today, and we are now on a very good road, heading for Sulphur Mountain. When we arrive, we get into the Banff gondola, which takes us by cable car 7500 feet up to the top. Wow!

Today we have the option of a helicopter ride over the mountains, or a visit to town. Try as I may, I could not get Rosie on that helicopter, and so there is just me, the pilot and two other tour members. The pilot says, "If you would like to talk to me, just press that button, and I sure did. I wanted to know so much, and he was so pleased to tell me all about his great country. Great guy. Looking down between my feet through the glass floor, I had a fantastic view. Glad I had the front seat. I had always disliked helicopters, but I could not resist this one; it was now or never. Unfortunately, the 30 minute trip had to be cut to 25, as the wind was picking up, and helicopters fliting between mountain peaks on a windy day was a little risky. Rosie had enjoyed her visit to Banff, and I had certainly enjoyed that helicopter trip. We were both highly pleased.

Now we are off to the Athabasca glacier. This is 23 square miles of snow and ice. When we arrived, we boarded a special coach and rove onto the glacier, but although it had been a lovely day, it changed instantly into a howling blizzard, and all we saw was snow. But what an experience.

Its day 7 and we are now in Jasper National Park, and our hotel will be the Jasper Inn. This is my kind of place. All the rooms are on the ground floor; same marvellous service with a smile, but quite different in its appearance. It has for me the look of the old frontier towns that I saw in the cowboy films. The winder rough roads, people moving casually about; no hurry and some of the people have an Eskimo appearance. All very friendly. When I said to Rosieta, "I think I could live here", she said, "Well you live here, and I will live in Toronto. Joking of course!"

Now here is something I must try! White water rafting. Rosie said, when I told her, "You must be joking!" I did not expect to get her on the raft, but I thought I would ask her. Rosie was quite content to meet me down river. There are ten of us sitting around the raft. We all have our yellow waterproof macs; we look like ten canaries. The white water covers the whole area, but now and again there is a much bigger rock, which of course would have us all in the river. There is where the guy with the sort of punt pole comes in. If we get near a big one he will push us away from it, but I am sure that when the raft turns full circle and we get a taste of the river, it is the guy with the pole making it a little more exciting!

About three miles down the river, we find our coach and all the guys get a big laugh seeing us in our yellow canary suits; and the thought that we actually thought that was fun, it was great. Rosie was also laughing and I was pleased about that. She did not seem to mind a bit that I wanted to try all these things, but to me it was a once in a lifetime things. I did not expect to be this way again.

This morning is ours just to wander, and Rosie and I are doing just that. The town of Jasper still had the appearance of the Gold Rush with its log cabins, the lumberjack-looking guys, the rough roads; one almost expected the Mounties to appear. I loved it! Now we board the 'Trans Canadian'; a powerful-looking train, quite a few coaches and another very powerful engine at the rear. This will take us back to Toronto airport for our flight home. We pass through Alberta, Saskatchewan, Manitoba, and it's still great. The lovely jade green Lake Louise, the rivers that have a very sky blue bed, due to what has been washed down from the Rockies, and now Niagara Falls.

Niagara is our last spectacular. We are given a light blue mac and we board the Maid of the Mist. This small steamer will take us as near as it can to the falls. I have seen it many times on TV but it is the absolute thunder that is produced by the water that makes this so impressive. Rosie and I are amazed and content. How we have seen it all, and next stop will be the airport. That will be tomorrow afternoon, but we still have tonight. Tonight we are going to the theatre where Rosie danced a few years ago, and we have treated ourselves to a taxi, and so we will arrive in style.

Rosie is so pleased as the ballet is her favourite. The one she saw at the school, Swan Lake. The theatre is packed and we are not too sure if we will get a ticket. We are in the theatre but not quite sure where the ticket office is and while we look around we see this very smart guy with his eyes firmly fixed onus. He seems not to be able to take his eyes off of us, and now here he comes! "Good evening, madam. I am awfully sorry to bother you, but could I have a few words with you, please? It is nothing serious, but something that I cannot get out of my mind". "Of course", Rosie said, "as long as I don't miss the ballet". "I assure you, ma'am, you will not do that, as I am the manager. You will have the best seat in the house. I have been watching you very carefully, almost mesmerised. You have an uncanny resemblance to a beautiful dancer of not so many years ago, when I was under manager and had the job of making sure that the girls did not have any undue hassle"

"The lady who to me you bare the extraordinary resemblance was the prima ballerina. Tell my, dear lady, are you Rosieta Rosalini? Please tell me." "You are absolutely right, Robert. My name is as you have thought, Rosieta Rosalini". He almost jumped up in the air, and laughed as he took Rosie's hands and she laughed, and I think people probably thought there were mad. "And you have remembered my name!" This is James, my very good friend. "Oh I do beg your pardon, sir", said

Robert the manager. He could see that Rosie was slightly displeased. "Now would you both please join me for the evening? It would be a great honour for me, and the theatre. "We would love to do that, Robert, wouldn't we James?" "We would indeed", said James, and Robert took Rosie's arm and we headed for what Robert had said would be the best seat in the house.

When we got to Robert's private box, he had four other guests, and proudly taking Rosie in, he said, "Now. Who can recognise this lovely lady?", and one gentleman stood up and said, "I can! The lady you have captured is that beautiful dancer, Rosieta Rosalini", and he moved forward, took Rosieta's hand and kissed it. "You have this evening, Rosieta, given me the chance to do what I have always wanted to do whenever I saw you dance: Kiss you, with your permission, sir, of course", he said as he turned to James. "It was a pleasure to meet you, sir" James said, "and to be here with you all, as guests of Rosieta's good friend Robert of years gone by", but not so many years that he had forgotten Rosieta, who could, and who would, ever want to. Rosieta is overwhelmed. I have never had much interest in ballet until I met Rosieta, but I would say tonight's performance was absolutely first rate. So much so that the ballet troupe received several standing ovations. The audience and our little group here, could I think have gone on and on. Fantastic!

Robert bids goodbye to his other guests, but not until the amorous gentleman has taken Rosieta's hand and given it a rather lingering kiss, while glancing at me with a little envy. I smile and say good night. Our evening is not yet over. Robert takes us into his office and opens the champagne. He has poured four glasses, but there are only three of us, but soon all is revealed. "It has been a wonderful evening, Robert, but I must ask you something that has occupied my mind, as you said I did, when you saw James and me. When I came to Canada on tour with my ballet troupe, there was a lovely girl by the name of Lorna; I think it was Lorna King. Do you know what happened to her? I think we all had an eye for Robert, but Lorna seemed to be determined to capture him, as she chased him round the room". Robert laughed, "Yes, I remember her. She changed her name you know." "Why would she do that?" Rosieta said. "Well," Robert said. "She married me!" Rosieta chuckled and said, "So she lives quite near?" "Yes" said Robert. I think I can hear her now", and Lorna appeared from their living quarters. Lorna and Rosieta wrapped their arms around one another. They hugged each other with a kiss on the cheek and, slightly watery-eyed, it was indeed a joy to see. Robert and I were also so very pleased, and we each raise a glass.

"I think we will leave you two gentlemen and go into the other room. There are a few things I would like to ask Rosieta alone. This made Jim think, but he was not going to ask what. Having lost the ladies, Jim and Robert were both anxious to know about each other. Robert got in first. "Jim, how did you meet Rosieta?" And the mere thought of it brought back that laugh again. He described their meeting at the supermarket and the rest of that extraordinary day, the lovely meal in the pub, and some of the things that had led up to this wonderful evening. "I think, Robert, it has given both Rosieta and I a new lease of life. I think neither Rosieta nor I would have dreamed of doing all that we have done on this holiday, had we not met. She is still so full of life and has given it to me. Of course, she can also be so annoying." "What's that?" said a voice in the other room. "Now Robert, working as you did with so many lovely ladies, I would like to know how Lorna performed better than the rest." "Mind how you answer that, Robert!" another voice from the other room. "I must admit, Jim, it was not the dancing. That was just part of my job. Although they were an exceedingly good ballet troupe, and Rosieta and Lorna were the best, and I am not just saying that because you are listening, Lorna!"

Rosieta and Lorna now emerge from the other room with wide grins. They had been listening and Robert and I had said some quite nice things, but we had said them because they both meant so much to us. "I hate to be the one to say it but we had better make a move if we are to be on that plane tomorrow. We would love to stay, but our holiday is over. But what a way to spend our last evening. Although I must say when I saw Lorna and Rosieta in that clinch, I did begin to wonder!" That did it! Lorna slowly come over to me, wrapped her arms round me, planted her lips on mine, and oh brother! I was glad to come up for air, phew! "Convinced now?" she said. "Well I am not quite sure" I said. "Could we do it again?" and we all laughed. "Well" Robert said. "I know Lorna quite well by now, but I don't know Rosieta very well. Shall we try one of those, Rosieta. No reply, just action! Wow!"

What an end to the day, and all four of us were wrapped around each other with not a work spoken for several minutes, just a few watery eyes. "It has been absolutely marvellous to have had you both with us" said Robert. "You are both very nice people, but it is also knowing what Lorna and Rosieta meant to each other, how they depended on each other while dancing, and we saw this evening how they did still do so value each other's friendship. Will you both please come back again?" "I think, Robert and Lorna, I can safely say that we will be back, and as I glanced at Rosieta there was no doubt we would be back.

Robert took Rosieta's arm, and Lorna took mine, and we slowly made our way to the taxi rank outside. Robert went to the taxi driven by his old friend, Charlie. He placed some cash in Charlie's hand and said, "Delta Chelsea" Charlie and after one more big hug and kiss, Charlie gently placed us in the car, and we waved as we bid goodbye to what had been a fantastic evening. The driver glanced into his mirror at a very happy couple.

"My name is Charlie" he said. "I have known Robert for many years. He used to tell me stories of what went on behind the curtain. He was so happy when he married one of those beautiful ballet dancers, but I think the one he would have liked to have landed was the prima ballerina, Rosieta Rosalini, but he said she was always slightly aloof. He thought her career came first to her. He we are" he said. "The Delta Chelsea. It has been a pleasure to meet two of Robert's friends. See you in England!" "Thank you, Charlie. Nice to know you."

I took Rosieta's arm and we slowly entered this hotel. It was a very large hotel and as our room was quite a number of floors up, I let Rosieta do the lifts. We entered our room and flopped down on the settee, exhausted, and after a few minutes I said to Rosieta, "How did you like the taxi driver's description of Rosieta Rosalini?" "No comment" she said. I think she was quite pleased in a way, but not of being described as aloof. I don't think I could see her that way.

Tomorrow we fly home, but the night is young. At least to Rosie, that is. I am beginning to wonder what makes her have these bursts of energy; our ages are only five years different. "Tomorrow, Rosieta, I would like to go to the Toronto Tower and look down through that glass floor. We don't have to go to the airport until the afternoon. Would you be up to it?" "Of course, Jim, but not tonight. I have other plans for tonight." "But it's nearly midnight, Rosie." "Oh Romeo, Romeo. Don't tell me you are weakening. Don't tell me that this last night in wonderland means so little to you. Come." And she takes his arm and closes the door.

Rosie slides out of bed in the morning with that same pixie grin, and heads for the bathroom, nodding her head with a thumbs up as she looks back at Jim, with a vitality that Jim has yet to find. It is a beautiful morning, the sun lights up all the skyscrapers, and standing out is the tower. "There we are, Rosie. All we have to do is keep our eye on the tower". Jim was a super optimist and he soon realised this. Our tour guide advised anyone going to the tower to go by taxi, but it is such a lovely morning and we would really live a good walk; even if Jim is now revitalised. And off we go.

We had not gone very far when Jim realised his plan would not work. The other skyscrapers had blotted out the tower, but a few very nice Canadians soon put us on track and we had arrived. It is a very tall building, but is has a very fast life and we are soon at the top with fantastic views, and a great restaurant, and a look down through that floor. Wow, it really hits you when you think what if that glass broke. But of course it is mighty thick. Well I enjoyed the walk and the trip up the tower, but I think we will have a taxi back! When we arrived back at the hotel, the tour guide was checking the luggage, and because she had been so good, I thought she deserved a few dollars. "Okay" Rosie said. "I will be in the hotel".

Debbie Swayze, the tour rep, was a smasher, and I thanked her for a good trip, and placed a few dollars in her hand, and she placed a lovely pair of lips on mine with a crushing hug and smile. Wow! Now that really was Canadian hospitality. I wonder what Rosie would have said.

Chapter Seven

End of a dream heading home

Debbie took us to the airport and gave us a little hug, and off we went to wait for our aircraft. The airport in Toronto was not quite the madhouse of Heathrow at least, as I saw it, that is. The homeward bound journey would not be quite as long as the outward bound, because the outward bound included the overland part across Canada from Toronto to Vancouver. This of course we have just done on the 'Trans Canadian' train. The flight of course was just as boring, and we touched down at Heathrow and joined the snaky queue to go through security. For some reason or another they searched my bag, and now to find our driver with our transport home.

The drivers seemed very interested in our holiday and I think we may have sold another Canadian vacation. It was good to get home. We had had a fantastic holiday, but it was still home. We flopped down on the settee and I said, "Rosie, I am shattered" and she looked at me with that impish grin of hers, "and it's not that" I said. And at that point the door to the dining room opened, and the family poured in. "Good gracious" said Rosie. What I said was a little less audible and unprintable, but I did my best to look pleased. After all, it was so good of them all to make the effort. We were hugged, shaken and kissed. They really were so pleased to see us looking so well.

Because we looked so well it prompted Jean to say to Jim, "If that's what the Rockies do for your weight, Jim, I think I will try some of that." and Rosie burst out laughing. Jean didn't think it was that funny, and so to cover it up Jim said, "Jet-lag, I think" and more laughter, and Jim made one last effort. "Richard and John, you did not tell me how much stamina your mother had" and that just produced another burst of high-pitched laughter from Rosie. "I was going to say, Rosie, that you had no trouble with those paths up in the Rockies. Come along, Rosie! Let's see what our good family have done in the dining room". The family were now putting two and two together and by their laughter, we coming up with the right answer.

In the dining room John said, "Where did you want her, Jim?" "You keep her with you, John. You will have more success controlling her than I would", and we all laughed. Having all got seated, conversation began to flow between bites, and Richard, being the youngest, had more of a sense of humour, much like his mother, and he said, "What exactly did you do in that vast wilderness?" It was rather unfortunate timing, as Rosie had her nose in the champagne, and of course she just had to laugh. The champagne is now spread over Rosie's spluttering face, and Sandra is mopping her up. Rosie still has a grin but is still spluttering, and I begin to answer to Richard's question. But first I want to say a few words about Rosie's laughter. "Have you recovered now, Rosie?" "Of course, Jim. No Problem."

And I continue, "Ever since she laughed with me in the trolley park, I have loved to hear her laugh. It is quite infectious. She seems to raise a laugh or a grin wherever she is, but of course it can sometimes be a little embarrassing. But even then it is amusing. Long may she laugh". And Jim raises his glass.

"Your question about hat vast wilderness, Richard, was, I think, designed to produce the laughter it did. But as has been said, laugh, and the world laughs with you. And we did. That wilderness is vast, but to me it was beautiful. Thousands of lovely dark green conifers, scattered among them the romantic Rockies, the jade green Lake Louise, sky blue rivers, vast, yes; but never daunting. Rather I would say, enticing. But Canada is also a country where the cities are bursting at the seams. Everywhere you look there is building going on. There is that dynamic feeling that this is a country that is going to succeed, and the people of that country could not be friendlier. And Richard, there are some lovely young ladies there, just waiting for some gallant Englishman to come riding into view. Well there you are, folks. I just had to say a few words about that lovely country. Now I think I had better get a little of this very nice food" and he received some light applause for his efforts.

Everything had gone so well – lovely food, champagne, good humour and conversation, but I think it must soon come to a conclusion. Time has marched on, but to my amazement Rosie stands up, "Jim has told you about wonderful Canada, and I know it means a great deal to him, geographically, and his knowledge of geology will make him want to return, bit I must tell you before you go off, what I shall always remember about our holiday." Rosie went on to tell them of that trip to the theatre, being spotted by the manager, who just had to ask her name, and her pride in saying 'Rosieta Rosalini', and being taken to the manager's personal box to see her favourite ballet 'Swan Lake'. "Never can I forget that wonderful evening, and it is all down to you. Had you not given Jim and I your personal blessing, he and I would never have experienced this fantastic second life, and Ron was right when he said it will be alright" Not just alright – absolutely fantastic. Thank you all."

It was so unusual for Rosie that we all gave her some real applause, and a few bravos. Needless to say that it brought a few tears to her eyes, but they were soon mopped up. John now stands and says how much they had all enjoyed the party, and hopes we can do it again soon. Jim's son, Ron, now thinks he should say a few words, and he says he thinks he will take Jean there for 'the slimming process'. The party has been marvellous. "But now Rosie and Jim, we had better be on our way". The usual hugs and kisses and departures, and all is quiet, and Jim and Rosie collapse onto the settee absolutely shattered.

It is a lovely morning and Rosie wakes Jim. "Jim, Jim, it is nine o'clock." When Jim finally wakes, he says, "Well what's the panic, Rosie? We are not going anywhere are we? After that marvellous holiday I think we deserve a lay-in." Jim of course knew that Rosie was a lady of routine. There was a time for everything, well most things. Some variations were justified! It was indeed a lovely morning, and after breakfast it was decided that a relaxing day in the garden would be nice.

Chapter Eight

Memories of Marjorie

"There is not much work that has to be done, Rosie, and so we will just do a tour, starting here with this lovely red camellia. This little nectarine tree is struggling to produce one nectarine. It would be nice, but it is unlikely. This lovely red rose is called 'Remembrance', a really beautifully formed rose with a gorgeous fragrance. The aconites and strawberries have long gone. Here we are at the sun house, where I would laze in the sun until I met you, Rosie. Now it is just great to sit with you, cheek to cheek, until I can persuade you to get the coffee. This large yellow conifer I bought in Woolworths for one shilling and sixpence fifty years ago. A yellow conifer was something I always wanted".

"This sweet-smelling shrub sometimes called 'Mock Orange' has of course finished for this year, and now we are in the orchard. The apples are Cox Orange, James Grieve and Russets; and the pear is Conference, and this is a Green Gage. This one is a peach, and this one is an apricot. That is all of the fruit in the garden, but we still have the grape in the greenhouse. This has about thirty bunches of beautiful black grapes. Just one snag:

they have pips. It is of course about forty years old. The figs are not ready".

Now inevitably of course, we wind up in the sun house and Jim asks Rosie if she would like a coffee, knowing of course that she will volunteer. While she was gone, he wandered round the garden again in his thoughts; mainly of Marjorie and the fifty seven years they had happily spent in this garden, and it almost brought tears to his eyes. That rose 'Thinking of You', the sun house, my special, the yellow conifer, the height of which worried her a little, her favourite herb, the red one, her fuchsias, the cianothus, lovely blue hibiscus, the yellow magnolia, and the red rhododendron Britannia that we bought to be a symbol of lasting love. And I see her in so many things as I walk around the garden, no matter how happy I am with Rosie; Marjorie I cannot, or would ever want to forget.

"Hello, Rosie. What kept you?" Some ladies might have poured it over me. She places it on the table and we snuggle up to each other, so happy that we found each other. I have never asked her about her previous loves. That is totally unimportant. We agreed to spend the autumn of our lives together, and nothing shall interfere with that. We never look back together. I only look back when I am alone, and I expect Rosie does the same. Nobody could reach their seventies and have no memories that they like to recall. We live for today. None of us knows how many days they have left, and that is good as we can still plan for the years ahead, and the happiness that there is still to be had.

Chapter Nine

Rosie loves parties

"Jim", Rosie says. "You have a birthday coming and I would like to have another get together to celebrate it." Jim does some quick calculations and says, "But that is a month away, and I am only just recovering from the last one." "Oh come on Jim, let's live a little, phew!" It's a good thing my insurance company doesn't know. They think I am just an old codger living all by myself." Rosie, determined as ever, organised the party and, to be honest, I also enjoyed it. There are always loads of laughs with a few embarrassing comments from one another. It is a great family now. It is almost time to call it a day, when the doorbell rings. "I'll go" says Jim. On opening the door there was a guy asking if he could have a few words with Rosieta. "My name is Ken Lynch". Rosie heard the name and called out "Come on in, Ken" and he comes through to the dining room. "Oh no no no, Rosieta. This can wait. You are enjoying your party". "You are here now" says Rosieta, "so let us deal with the problem.

Rosieta turns to the family and says, "Ken is one of the few remaining newspaper men whose stories are based on the truth. What's the problem, Ken? How can

I help you?" "Well, Rosieta. It is a case of me wanting to help you, if I can, and with your help I think I can. You recently had a very nice evening in Toronto at the theatre, and a very nice guy on the city paper wrote a glowing tribute to you, with pictures of you from your dancing years. You really did come over beautifully. Unfortunately, the paper also has a gossip columnist with one of the worst muck papers, who thinks that behind the lovely Rosieta Rosalini there must be some much to be found an so he contacted a fellow mucker in this country. The guy in the country has asked me if I can find out anything about your sister, Phyllis, and by going through Phyllis, he thinks he can get at you, and your beautiful image which I think you so well deserve; and I intend to destroy this mucky story before it begins. This is what I would like to do. I did not know that you had a sister, Rosieta, but if you could give me a few details about her I think I could weave such a beautiful story around her that no muck paper would find her of any interest, and the story would be no more. What do you think, Rosieta?"

Rosie went forward looking down at the floor, head in her hands. Not a word was said for a few minutes, and then she looked at Ken and spoke, "Ken" she said, "my sister deserves all the notoriety she gets, but I will not allow her to destroy me in the same way as she seems so keen to destroy herself. I have worked hard in my career, but she who was a beautiful young lady, just used that beaut to destroy any man that was attracted to her, and there were many. I will tell you what she did last year, but it is a long story, Ken. How much time do you have?" "If I can kill this mucky story before it begins" he said, "then I have all the time in the world."

"How about you, my family? Do you want to hear it? It is an uncanny, almost ghostly story" "We would like to stay, Rosie. Please go on". And Rosie begins.

Phyllis was a beautiful young lady, with all the right measurements. She was a magnet for all the men in the area. She just chewed them up and spat them out, until she met Fred. Fred was a plantsman. He scoured the world looking for rare and exotic plants that garden centres could make a fortune on. His favourite area was Nepal. He had a cabin up in the mountains, and he told Phyllis about it. The dreamy scatter-brained Phyllis soon persuaded Fred to take her there. He did not know it, but my dear sister was about to destroy him too.

Having got herself nicely settled into Fred's cabin, she sent us an invitation to visit them. It sounded quite idyllic, and I and my brother jumped at the chance. William, my brother, and I flew to Kathmandu in Nepal, the nearest we could get to Fred's cabin. "There is the cabin up there" said the driver. "Sorry I can take you no further". "Thank you" we said. We started up the long winding path; every step produced a cloud of dust. With only about one hundred yards to go, we were getting flashes from a mirror, and a voice says, "Come on up". It was my scatter-brained sister. We now became aware of the couple behind us, Bill and Pauline, who we had met on the plane, but would rather not meet again. But we were all heading for the spider's web."

Rosie and I had met and exchanged greetings with Phyllis and Fred, when Fred's plantsman friend from a little further down the path appeared. He was a tall, good-looking guy with a smile from ear to ear. He looked so pleased to see Fred's visitors, until he saw Pauline and Bill, who were just approaching. His gaze fixed on Pauline, as if there was a gigantic magnet drawing them together, until he blurted out, "Sorry, I must go. I have forgotten something", and he stumbled off down the path. He fell in his haste to get away. He had the appearance of a man who did not care if he did fall over the side into the ravine. The man with that wonderful smile was devastated.

Pauline now jumps up and says, "I must go to him. He is not well". She was desperate to get to Keith before he injured himself. She seemed to give not a thought to her own safety as she stumbled over the rocky path. Two hours later they had not returned, and this was worrying Fred. HE began to wonder if either of them had reached Keith's cabin, and he said, "I must go and see if they are alright." When Fred go to Keith's cabin, all was well. Keith and Pauline were in each other's arms, and vowing never to part again. "Hello, Fred. Thanks for coming down. Come in for a few minutes" and in that few minutes Fred thought what a tangled web we do weave. Keith and Pauline were in fact husband and wife. They parted four years ago, but neither of them felt that they wanted divorce, and now the reason was obvious. "I will be getting from now" said Fred. "I just wondered if you were okay. "Thank, Fred. We will see you in about half an hour" and Fred made his way along what seemed like a long, lonely path.

When we arrive back at his shack, there was no sign of Phyllis. "Where is Phyllis?" he said. "Oh" said William. "She has taken Bill to see the village. "Oh well" said Fred, "We will have a cup of tea, shall we?" And that was the last we saw of Phyllis and Bill. We learned later that they had known each other very well before, and it was quiet clear that they would not be seeing Fred again. Phyllis can cross Fred off. Another man destroyed.

It seemed as if Phyllis had some kind of hate for all men, with her charming ways and beautiful figure, she could threat them almost like puppets. They would dance at the ends of her strings until she decided she was tired of them, and cut the strings. Next day, William and I decided that the day would only get worse, and they asked Fred if there was a plane out of Nepal today. "Yes" he said "there is one at midday." "Well Fred, I think we will be on it. Sorry how things have turned out, Fred." Phyllis, my sister, has done what she has done so many times. She has no feeling for others, just her own selfish self, and she has destroyed so many lives in the process. I hope Fred you can put her out of your life. She is just trouble for everyone. Fortunately, Keith and Pauline have arrived, and they are obviously over the moon, and they quickly change the atmosphere with an explanation of their reunion, of how stupid arguments brought about four years of unhappiness, and how they would not allow it to happen again.

Sadly, as William and I are about to go, Keith and Pauline will return to Keith's cabin and Fred will be alone with his plants, thinking of my bitch of a sister. I hope he soon forget her. "We will be off now, Fred" and Rosie gave him a big hug and a kiss. I shook his hand with a firm grip and we moved to Keith and Pauline, with hugs and kisses, and Rosie whispers to them, "You will look after him" and they nodded. William and I set off down the winding track, turning to wave now and again until we reach the bottom, and we are out of sight. The idyllic holiday in the Nepalese hills just never happened. We have come all this way, only to see a very nice guy destroyed by my own sister, and I ask myself how could she be so different from William and me.

I felt there was some ghostly intent in it all. Had Phyllis worked it all out? Did she intend to destroy the more successful member of the family, to bring them down to her level? Phyllis was a beautiful young woman, and still is a beautiful woman. She could capture any man, but she lacks the common sense to hold onto him. I have called her a bitch, but I pity her. I don' know where she is now and I don't want to". "I do" said Ken. "Well don't tell me, Ken. My sister is trouble." "I will do, as I have said, Rosieta. I will weave a wonderful story around Phyllis, one that no muck-raking columnist would touch. It will not be so difficult as she now works with the very needy, the blind and disabled, and those with dementia. She does seem to be a changed woman.

Chapter Ten

Rosie has a sister again

With those last few words, Ken had given Rosieta a completely different picture of Phyllis, and a feeling of intense compassion came over her, and as I have said, Rosieta is a lovely, warm-hearted woman and she felt that she might still help her sister. Rosieta turned to Ken and asked him if he would just jot down where Phyllis is now. "I really ought to know, as her next of kin". "There you are, Rosieta, but stand well back to be here sister" and off her went. The family now prepared to go. "What a story, Rosieta". "Yes" she said "and what makes it worse is that it is all absolutely true. Phyllis has been a bitch, but after those last words of Ken, I don't feel I can write her off completely. She does seem to be a changed woman." The family are a little concerned. "Do as Ken says, Rosieta. Wait a while, see what you hear, and if the changed woman lasts then go to her and be that sister that she longs to see, but you must be sure." "Thank you, my family. That is, I think, good advice, and Jim and I thank you all for coming. But I am sorry that my story took up all the time in which we were going to tell you all about the holiday, but we will do it again." With the usual hugs and kisses, they go on their way, and as independent as we are, it still felt good to have a reliable family.

A month has passed and it has worried me a great deal to see Rosie so quiet, so fidgety, unable to concentrate. It was a relief when she said, "Jim. I am going to find Phyllis tomorrow. I feel I must know, is she or is she not this changed woman?" This morning Rosie has phone the home and spoken to the matron running it, asking "Would it be convenient to see Phyllis, my sister? I have been told she works with you". "You must be Rosieta. Oh that's wonderful; please do come along this afternoon. She will be so keen to see you." "Just one thing" said Rosie, "please do not tell her I am coming. I must see her reaction when she first sees me. I will explain that later." "I won't say a word, Rosieta. My name by the way is Angela. Bye for now".

When we arrived at the home for the disabled, I parked the car a small distance from the main door, and I suggested to Rosie that she remains in the car while I go and find Angela, the matron. On entering, Angela approached me and I told her that I had left Rosieta in the car, so that Phyllis could meet her alone. "I see" said Angela "I will call Phyllis. Angela directed Phyllis to me and I said I was her driver, and Rosieta was in the car. "She is waiting for you, Phyllis" and off she went so excited. I watched, and Angela watched; both of us I think near to tears.

As Phyllis grew near, Rosie gets out of the car and they paused, looked at each other, wrapped their arms around each other with beaming smiles, and tears running down their cheeks. And now Angela and I wipe our eyes. Angela and I wait just inside to give Rosieta and Phyllis as much time as they needed, for this was no ordinary meeting. So much depended on it. The door opens and two very happy ladies enter, and we stand up and all four of us are now wrapped around each other. Words were rather in short supply. Angela steps forward, takes Rosie's hand and thanks her for coming to the home. "I have heard a lot about you, and all good I may add." "Thank you, Angela" and Rosieta moves nearer to me. "This is my good friend, James. You have met Angela, Jim, and this is my lovely sister, Phyllis." And I have a hug and a kiss, and for the life that Phyllis had led according to Rosie, Phyllis was still a very interesting lady. I hope they will both remain good sisters.

As we move towards Angela's office, we can see about a dozen patients where they pass the day, which I expect is often long. These patients are only in the early stages of dementia, and could hold a reasonable conversation, but it also meant they could remember so much that would make them want to go home. Angela the matron has her eye on Jim, who does seem quite interested in the situation, and another volunteer would always be acceptable. "Jim" she says, "do you think you could go round this little group and just ask their names and where they come from? It would mean to much to them. They see so very few people. Although they are together, it is still a rather lonely life for them." "But I have never done anything like that, Angela. I would be lost for words." Rosieta did a chuckle. "I have never known it. Go on, Jim. Make their day." "Oh well, I will give it a go."

I opened the door and their faces lit up like I was a well-known film star. Angela, Phyllis and Rosieta went into the matron's office. Now I was in the deep end.

I passed time with the first two ladies and then I came to the only man in the group, and he stood up and said "I am Pierre. I am French. I am from France." "Ah, bonjour, Monsieur Pierre. Parlez-vous Anglais?" His French, like mine, was practically non-existent, and so he began to sing the French national anthem. I like the French anthem; it has really got some punch behind it, so I join him. We sing it with gusto, we punch the air in a defiant gesture, with expressions on our faces that would leave any enemy in no doubt we will fight to the end and we would win! And when we came to the end, I said loud and clear, "Vive la France"" but I realised I had taken a little too much out of Pierre, and I sat him down and he whispered, "Vive la France", but he had a lovely contented, victorious expression on his face. I shook his hand and said, "Au revior, Pierre."

I moved to the next person. She was quite a lively lady and I said, "You must be Joan of Arc." "Non" she said, "I am Marie Antoinette". The next lady did not wait to be asked. She proudly announced that she was "Madame Lafayette". The next two ladies were quite hysterical. They were laughing so much they could hardly tell me who they were, and then they shouted at the top of their voices, "We're from Bermondsey, mate!" Now that had me laughing, and I said it was good to be back in England and London. The next lady left me a little sad. She was quite a refined lady and she said, "I live in Tenterden." "That's a lovely area" I said. "Yes, it is" she said. "Do you know when I shall be going home?" "Well" I said, "you will have to ask the matron that." "Yes, of course" she said. "Of course." The last lady said, "I am Jean. I live in Ashford." "That's nice" said Jim. "I know it well".

He had been all round and he had really quite enjoyed it, although he was still a little concerned about Pierre. He was, of course, as English as myself, but if he wanted to be French, well it would hurt nobody. People in these homes have so little. I opened the door to go and turned to my new friends and said "Goodbye. I will come again." On entering the matron's office, there was no shortage of conversation, but the matron, Angela, said, "What was all that singing about?" "It was the Frenchman, Pierre, being patriotic, and it spread to me. It made my day, Angela." Pierre had been a real man again, a fighting man, a Legionnaire, just for a few minutes, and when he sat down the look on his face said, "the battle has been won" and I was proud that I had stood beside him. I know he is as English as me, but that does not matter. He had been happy, but I would like you to look at him. I think it took a lot out of him. "I will do that, Jim, and when I come back I would like to show you the grounds. Would that be okay, Rosieta?" "I think I might allow that" she said." "He is okay, Jim. He has recovered now. Let us go for that walk." And as she takes my arm, "Mind what you get up to" said Rosieta. "What, at my age?" said Jim. "I am well aware of your capabilities" said Rosieta.

Jim knew why Angela wanted to take him for a walk, and what her first question would be. "How did you meet Rosieta, Jim?" "Well, Angela. There was nothing romantic about it. In fact, I was very much annoyed with her. I like to go into the store in and out quickly. Rosieta was having great difficulty in removing her trolley and holding me up. Seeing my frustration, she laughed and this made me a little angry, but shortly afterwards in the manager's office over a glass of champagne I did learn of her name, Rosieta Rosalini, and after the manager's toast, she accompanied me to my home with the manager's secretary. From there on, Angela, it has been a fairy tale. We are both very happy with our second life, which we see as the autumn of our lives, and we are both determined to live them to the full. Well there you are then, Angela. Is that anywhere near what you had imagined?" "No, Jim. It is not, but it is wonderful. How I envy you both, in your seventies and starting a new life in good health, with the world at your feet."

"I have told you of our fairy tale life, Angela, but please do not let it take over your imagination. What you are doing here is so much more important. As I was going round your patients, I said to myself, "There but for the grace of God go I." In their situation, they do so need caring people like you and Phyllis. Don't let them down, Angela. Rosieta and I could be there one day. None of us knows. Now what about you, Angela? How did you get to be in control here? Are you able to turn off at the end of the day? Do you think about what will happen to your patients as their dementia takes hold?" "I was a nurse in a local hospital and I had very nearly reached the top, and fancied a change and this was just right. I do sometimes worry about the patients but my nursing training does enable me to turn off. This, of course, a nurse in any situation must do. Well, Jim. I have very much enjoyed your company, but I think we ought to be getting back" and with that I was rewarded with a nice kiss, which of course to be polite I returned.

When we arrived back at the office, Rosie said "Did he behave himself?" And Angela said, "Absolutely impeccably, unfortunately" and that produced a laugh all round. Would you mind, Rosieta, if I took a stroll with Jim?" said Phyllis. "No" said Rosieta. "Then perhaps I could have one, all in good humour, of course" and Phyllis takes my arm and I get my second stroll. I am so glad to get you on your own, Jim. There is so much I would like to ask you. How are you getting on with my big sister? Has she told you much about me?" "Up until a month or two ago, I did not know you existed, Phyllis. She had never mentioned you, but Rosieta had a visit from a newspaper reporter, and that changed everything. A muck-raking reporter in Canada had asked a fellow muck-raker in England to dig up all the muck he could on Phyllis, that they might be able to use it to blacken the image of the lovely Rosieta, but her friend on the local paper was determined this would not happen".

"The Phyllis we came to know was the lady in Nepal; the beautiful young lady with all the right measurements, who devoured any man, including Fred, and spat them out without a thought for any of them. We were told that she is a beautiful woman, and they were not wrong, but Rosieta did not want to risk what the muck-raker would so love to do. But a few words from her reporter friend changed all that, when he said, "I think she is a changed woman now". He told us what your life entailed now and in our minds, we could see what it could mean to the unfortunate souls in your car, but still Rosieta was afraid to risk it. A month has gone by, and I could see what it was doing to Rosieta. She could not concentrate. She was all on edge, and eventually she said, "I must go and see Phyllis, Jim" and I was so pleased that the meeting was going to happen at last."

"Well, Phyllis. Have you any doubt as to just how she feels about you? Are you that changed woman? Will you be Rosieta's sister again? Tell me, Phyllis, what are your thoughts now? Rosieta has come to mean a great deal to me. I could not bear to see her hurt." "I am that changed woman, Jim. When I look back now, I find it difficult to believe that I was that woman that you have been told of, but I know I was; and while I cannot change the past, the woman you see now is that woman I will be to the end of my days." I gave her a big hug and said, "You have made my day, Phyllis. I was, like Rosieta, a little concerned that the changed woman might not last, but I am quite sure now that Rosieta has a sister again. Welcome back, Phyllis."

We carried on with our walk, and she told me of the patients she had seen go through the home, and at times, I thought her tears were not far away. I don't think I could do it, but perhaps a woman has a great deal more compassion than a man. "They do some funny things at times, Jim, and we do have a laugh. But it is with them, not at them, and I am sure they know the difference." "Well, Phyllis, I think we should return to the other ladies." "Yes, Jim. You are right. But before we go, I must thank you so much. You have, I think, made it quite impossible for me ever to be the woman I was, and for that, and I get a real smacker. "Wow" I said. "I am glad I came". The kiss she gave me had no other motive; I am sure, other than a very warm thank you. But of course I was equally thankful, because I felt so reassured that Phyllis really would live up to her words, and Rosieta would have a loving sister again.

When we arrived back with the ladies, still with Phyllis' arm in mine, Rosieta said, "Well, hello. You must be feeling quite tired, Jim." And we all laughed and did one of our hugs. It had been a wonderful time and we headed for the door. Rosieta and Phyllis now have an arm round the other, and I was so pleased to see it; the family together again. "Now don't forget" said Angela to Jim, "If you ever have time on your hands, we would be very glad to see you again." "Thank you" he said "but I really don't think I could do it like you ladies. My half an hour today was nothings like the amount of work you all have to do, and I have the greatest admiration for you all for doing it." After making sure that phone numbers and addresses are all recorded, we head for the car, and with the usual hugs and waves we are on our way home, and so happy that we have made the effort.

A month has gone by and all seems to be well with Phyllis and Rosieta, and as happy as Rosieta was, she does now seem even more so. But she now has been given a problem that could affect the whole family. And today she probably will have to decide on a very important family matter. Richard has asked if he can bring his new lady to visit this afternoon; quite ironic really when I think of it. When Rosieta and I came back from Canada, I said to Richard, "There are some lovely young ladies in Canada, just waiting for a handsome young man to come riding over the hill." Little did I know, but she was already here, and that Richard and Debbie were quiet well acquainted. Here they are and as they walk up the drive they look a fine couple. She is about the same height, with all the right measurements. I think there are going to be some difficult questions to which, inevitably, Rosieta will have to say yes. Rosie gets a good hug when she opens the door and Richard introduces Debbie to Rosieta and me; I just could not help thinking what a lucky swine Richard was. We sit them down and provide the refreshments, and after the customary polite comments, Richard opens the conversation.

"I had to smile to myself, Jim, when you mentioned the lovely young Canadian ladies on your return from Canada, but I had not known Debbie long and I was not sure how I stood with her. But I am very pleased to say now I am quite sure and that is, of course, why we must discuss what we have in mind. Debbie now has her degree in geology and the mining company that has sponsored her is looking forward to her return to Canada. There is not great urgency, but of course we know that she now has to work in their laboratories. When Debbie does go back to Canada, mum, I would like to be with her, and if all goes well, we would like to be married in her home on the Prairie. "Well it sounds quite lovely, but what do your parents say, Debbie?" "I had about half an hour on the phone to them and they were quite excited. They were so happy about my degree, and now I had also found the man of my dreams. Mother of course is an incurable romantic, and is just entranced by the thought of a lovely wedding. Father, however, wanted to know a little more about Richard, but I had no trouble convincing him that I was making the right choice."

"I have my job with this large mining company. There is no problem there, and I am absolutely sure Richard will have no problem. Canada is a hive of industrial activity. In all the big cities there is a massive building program going on. If you can give Richard and me your blessing on our plans to marry, then we would like you both to fly over for the wedding. That would be so lovely. I think now I will leave you two to have a little chat together, while Jim takes me for a walk round the garden. It does look so nice out there. Is that okay?" "That's fine" says Richard. "How about you, Jim?" "How could I refuse such an invitation?" and I took her arm with a grin. It was a very nice thought of Debbie's. Rosieta is going to lose her youngest son, and Debbie being a woman could imagine just how that might feel, but I think she knew that Rosieta would never stand in his way. She would want him to have all the chances she had.

"You mentioned home on the Prairie, Debbie. Just what do your family do?" "Well, Jim. You had that Canadian holiday, and you came back across the country; you must have passed through the Great Grain Belt, Alberta, Siscaturan, Manitoba, and my family live in Alberta, where my father has a great many acres of grain and a lovely house. But it is out in the middle of nowhere, but we love it. Have you ever been on a horse, Jim?" "No, I have not." "Well" says Debbie, I think I have just the one for you when you come over". Jim is beginning to feel his age! It always looks a long way down form a horse, but he had to admit, it did all sound most exciting.

Having been all round the garden, we sit down in the sun house and continue our conversation, mostly on Canada. "I did find the Great grain growing areas most interesting, Debbie, but it was the huge coniferous areas that really impressed me. It seemed to me I had space to breathe, with peace and quiet." "Well, Jim. There is a nice bungalow just up the road from us." "How far is it just up the road, Debbie?" Said Jim. "Oh not more than twenty five miles, I would say." "That's what I thought" he said, "because your country is so big, distance does not matter to a Canadian." "But you would love it, Jim. It sits in about fifty acres of conifers." "What would I do with all that?" said Jim. "You would call me, and I would see what we under them. You could be sitting on a uranium mine. Of course you would not want to stay there, but the value would be immense. You would just live it up on the proceeds!"

"Hello hello" calls a voice. Rosieta and Richard have come to join us, and having sat themselves down, Rosieta says, "And what have you been saying to Debbie, Jim?" "Well, it is really what has Debbie been saying to me? Debbie just told me about this nice house just up the road from where she lives. It has a lovely big garden about fifty acres. How much?! And it would be no good nipping round for a bowl of sugar, because it is twenty five miles up the road"" "Well, Jim. If you could join me in wishing this happy couple a very happy married life." Jim jumped up and Debbie did likewise. A big hug and a kiss, and Jim said, "I certainly will, although it makes me so envious. They are young, fully of energy, and have so much to look forward to, but in that married life I hope they will always remember that port of a marriage so often forgotten; compromise. I wish you both all the happiness in the world" and we had a hug.

Rosieta had been to see John and Sandra, to put them in the picture. Debbie and Richard have also been and it all is set for a very happy occasion. We shall await the final arrangements. It is two weeks now since we met Debbie with Richard. She seems in no rush. I think she has developed a great liking for England, as well as Richard. But they fly to Canada the day after tomorrow. Richard is now with his mother. Debbie has a little more to attend to. "Well, mother. Thank you for your blessing on our wedding. Debbie thought you were lovely, and Jim was great fun. The arrangements are now quite advanced and we would like it to be in three weeks' time. But we would like you and Jim to come over to Canada in about a week to give you both a holiday as well as to be with the family. Would you be happy to do this?" She paused for a moment, and she reflected on the time she met Jim. They were behaving like teenagers and enjoying every day, but now each day reminds her that time marches on. That does not mean, of course, that she will cease to be that lovely ballerina, Rosieta Rosalini. She will dance as long as she can; now of course just for herself.

I think that would be very nice, Richard. That sounds lovely, but I think we ought to call Jim. He is in the garden. "Jim, could you come in for a moment?" "What's up, Rosie? Oh hello, Richard. How long have you been here?" "Not long, Jim, but we have been discussing the wedding and I have just asked mum if she would come over to Canada a couple of weeks before, as a little holiday, as well as to be with us. How would you feel, Jim?" "That sounds great, Richard, but what did Rosie say?" "I too think it would be lovely" she said. "That's marvellous" Richard said, as he jumped up and took our hands with a big hug. "Thank you both. You have made it all even more wonderful. Now the next time we meet, it will be in Canada, and we will all be looking forward to that time. I know Debbie's mother and father are just dying to meet you both. And with a hug and a wave he was gone, leaving a very quiet and thoughtful Rosie. We have informed the rest of the family what is planned and they seemed pleased for everyone; the happy couple, and ourselves, enjoying a very nice holiday.

Chapter Eleven

Rosie's Canadian Grandson

Here we go. We have hired a taxi to Heathrow. We know the airport routine now, but it does take a rather long time these days, and we will be glad to get the weight off our legs. On the aircraft, but I am now looking forward to seven boring hours of the flight. I would like to sleep, but I never seem able. We are going to fly to Toronto and do the rest by train. I don't really like flying. At Winnipeg, Debbie will meet us and we do the rest by road. I do find the size of this country a little overpowering, but the people are great. All goes well. We land at Toronto, which is not quite so big as Heathrow, and I am pleased about that. Loads of taxis and all speaking that great language, English, and we are on the train and hoping that Debbie will be at Winnipeg to meet us. As I have said, this country is so big and to me a little overpowering.

We pull into Winnipeg and there she is. What a sight for sore eyes; Debbie beaming all over. She gives me a big hug and a smacker, and Richard has his arms around his mum. All change and Debbie gives Rosie a great hug and kiss, and I shake Richard's hand. It has all the promise of a very happy time. Debbie and Richard now take us to the local hotel, and over a meal and a drink, Richard says, "Now I hope you don't mind, folks, but we have booked rooms here for the night, and we will go on tomorrow. We still have quite a long way to go. Whatever you want, just ask. You will do that, won't you?" "Yes, we will." By the time we left our room, Debbie and Richard had settled the bill and were waiting in the lounge. They rose as we approached. Another hug and they asked if we had slept well, and off to the car. "Now we have quite a way to go" they said "but it is beautiful country, and I think it will keep you awake. But if it doesn't, don't worry. We will not mind."

Well it was a hell of a long journey, and we did drop off, and when we awoke it was in from of this very large house, and approaching us now, almost running, was a lovely lady with a grin from ear to ear. She doesn't wait for Debbie. She takes hold of the car door handle, opens the door, and almost pulls Rosie out with one quite enormous hug. I think they will get on fine! "As you might possibly have imagined" said Debbie "this is my mother. Her name is Beatty and she is marvellous. This gentleman, mum, is Jim. I have told you all about him and as you can see, I did not exaggerate. He's a great guy. Having gathered us up, Beatty takes us to the kitchen. There, in the centre of a very large room, was a very large table. It was a table of years gone by. Solid oak, not lacquered. But it had the sheen of years of hard work. We had a very welcome cup of tea, and through the course of conversation, it was quite obvious that Beatty was a very happy woman in a house she really loved.

We discussed the trip etcetera, and inevitably the conversation got around to the wedding. "I would like to show you the house, Rosieta, and of course your room." At that point, Richard remembered he had a job outside. "Would you like to come, Jim?" "Yes, Richard. See you later, ladies. Okay, Richard." "Thought you would prefer to be out her than discussing the domestic situation, Jim." "Thank you, Richard. Well done." We walked round the rather large garden and through a bank of conifers, and then it was clear for as far as the eye could see. This was Debbie's father's grain empire; all three thousand acres of it. "Does it ever scare you a little, Richard? That one day you might be called upon to take control of all this?" "The thought had crossed my mind, Jim. But when you have known Debbie a little longer you will see a woman who would be afraid of nothing, and together there would be no problem we could not control. When you meet her father tonight, when he comes home, you will see where he gets it from. Frank is a guy who would allow nothing to beat him. I like him and I think he has in the back of his mind that his future son-in-law is going to be Frank mark two. There is no big stick with Frank. He just seems to be a born leader of men. I think you will like him also, Jim. Now we had better join the ladies.

On entering the house, Rosieta hears us, and she calls out, "Jim, come up and see this beautiful room Beatty has given us." Richard chuckled and went through to the kitchen. "See you, Jim." It was indeed very nice. Lovely Beatty. We shall be sorry to go home. Debbie hears Jim and calls out, "Well there is always that little place up the road." "Do you mean the old Roberts' place?" "Yes, I mentioned it before I left England." "I don't think Rosieta would want to be there on her own" said Beatty. "One thing's for sure, Jim" said Debbie. "The view would be the same, just conifers" and they all had a good laugh. "I will leave you to unpack your things and I will check on the dinner. That sounded great, but Beatty need not have worried. Debbie had taken control, and I could see just what Richard mean; she was going to be an absolute treasure; beautiful, with a brain to match.

We hear the sound of a vehicle and Frank's Land Rover is in the yard. I am really looking forward to meeting him. He enters the kitchen, kicks his boots off and quickly comes to find his guests. He comes into the lounge. "Good evening, all" and takes a firm hold of Rosieta, gives her a big smacker, puts her at arm's length and has a good look at her. You have not changed much. Still the beautiful Rosieta Rosalini. Do you still dance?" "Not now, Frank. Not in public anyway. They had never met, but Frank had seen her dance onstage a few years ago, and just could not wait to meet her. "Well, if you have quite finished welcoming Rosieta, Frank, I would like to introduce her very good friend, Jim, and we all laughed as Frank put his hand out. "Great to meet you, Jim. You are not going to take a swipe at me, are you?" "No, Frank. Everyone reacts the same when they meet Rosieta. So many people have seen her dance and fallen in love with her; the way I met her bore no resemblance to her theatrical life, but our second life has been wonderful, and as he looked across at Rosieta, there was some gentle applause.

"Now have you still got an appetite after all that, Frank?" said Beatty with a grin. "I certainly have" he said. "Now what is it to be" as he slipped his arm around her. "Roast pork with all the trimmings." "Great,

I'll get washed up." Canadians must have very good appetites. I was never going to eat all that lot, but it smelled and looked so good. Well here goes and it was as good as it looked and although I was a little behind the rest, I did manage to eat the lot. It may have been just for the guests, but it was followed by a lovely apple pie and wine. Plenty of wine and plenty of conversation. Frank wanted to know about Great Britain, and I was very much interested in Canada. It was a very pleasant evening, but I was feeling very tired. Perhaps it was the wine, but I asked my hosts if they would mind if I had an early night. Rosieta said that she too would retire, "But before we do, we thank you for a marvellous welcome, with you very pleasant personalities. You suggested a holiday. We look forward very much to the days ahead, good night." They were still in full flow as we went to our room, but we were absolutely whacked.

In the morning we felt fine. The family were all up and ready to go. "I would like to take you round the ranch today, Jim." said Frank. "Oh no" said Debbie, "I wanted to take him for a ride on an Old Swifty". "Okay, Debbie. We will go tomorrow, alright Jim?" "Alright, Frank. I shall look forward to it." "Have you ridden on a horse before, Jim?" "No, I have not" and Frank went off with a chuckle. "You will be fine" said Debbie. We went over to the stable and I was near to declining the invitation, but I was introduced to this lovely old horse, so calm and docile that I thought anyone could ride him. Debbie gets him out and calls to Richard, "Can you help Jim up?" "A pleasure" he said, and between them I was in position. I felt like suggesting they tied me on, but I thanked them and Debbie gets her horse and is quickly in the saddle. She looked a real picture.

"Okay, Jim?" "As ready as I'll ever be, I reckon." Richard laughed. "You'll be fine, Jim." said Debbie. "Off we go. Where's the starter, Debbie?" "Oh just give him a gentle kick in the ribs and say 'come on Swifty'. He will start" and he did. We moved at a gentle pace and headed off into the conifers. Debbie was great. She seemed to know when to chat and when to let me soak up this wonderful silence, listen to the unusual bird calls, breathe this clean, pure air. I was really enjoying it. She looked across and smiled; I think she too was so happy. We turned after about a couple of miles, and after a while, we left the conifers and came upon Frank's pride and joy. For as far as the eye could see, there was the gently moving wheat, and oars, swaying in the breeze and we stopped; and it was silent for a few minutes. "There you are, Jim. That is what frank, my dad, does from daylight to dark. He loves it. This is his empire. I am sure at the end of the day he is well pleased with his labour. The men who work for him think he is great. He expects every man to work as hard as himself, but he rewards them very well."

"I have just one concern, Jim. Will he expect my Richard to work as hard as himself? I don't think anyone would or could. It is his empire that drives Frank on, and I would love them both." "I don't think you need to worry, Debbie. I am sure Frank realises that he himself puts in 110% and he would not expect quite that commitment from those who worked with him. He is a great guy." We turn and head back to the house and it has been a very pleasant experience. I might get one of these; perhaps on with a self-starter. Back in the yard, Richard and Debbie help me down. "How did it go" said Richard with a grin. "It was marvellous, Richard.

I enjoyed the air, the scenery, and the very pleasant company. And I would like to do it again." Beatty was a little concerned, knowing I had never ridden a horse, but I assured her that I enjoyed it, and I had a good instructor; and I guess Frank was laughing to himself as he worked.

The next day, it was Frank's turn to see my reactions. I was doing things I could never have dreamed of, and of course I was not too confident, but I would always have a go. "Okay" says Frank. Come on, Jim. I am going to show you around."

Chapter Twelve

The Horse Ride was great. Now what?

Frank is looking into the mirror, probably to see if he has egg on his face, and Jim did not see it, but Debbie was doing the sign of the cross on her chest while Richard laughed. "I saw that in the mirror, Debbie." "Sorry, Dad. Just a joke." "That will do, Debbie" says mum. "Did I miss something, says Jim. "Nothing of any importance" says Frank. "Come on, Jim." And I was into the Land Rover, but not for long. Out of the yard round the first lot of wheat and there was a long grassy strip, at the end of which stood a light aircraft. Frank was watching Jim for his reaction. "Holy smoke, Frank. Have you any more surprises for me? Can you fly this?" And he pulls out of his pocket his pilot's licence. "A horse would not be much good for what you will see today, Jim. You gonna trust me, Jim? Come on, climb aboard, Jim." "Aren't we supposed to have parachutes, Frank?" "No, they would not be much good at the height we travel at, but we could glide down quite well, plenty of room to land."

Jim was not too sure of things, but he was not going to have it said that he was too scared to fly with Frank, and he sat in the co-pilot's seat. Just to put the wind up Jim a little more, Frank said that he had the other set of controls put in in case he should collapse while flying, then the other man could take it down. That did not improve Jim's confidence, but he was not going to show it. Frank's grass-stripping runway was mighty bumpy, and with all his concern, Jim was glad to be airborne. "We are off the ground now, Jim. How are you feeling?" "Strangely enough, Frank, I feel a little more at ease." "By the time we come home, you will want to fly it, Jim. It's exciting being totally in control, jumping over everything." The little plane did not lead into the air like those big jets, and it took a while to reach its cruising height, but when it had, it was great. No other vehicles to worry about, visibility for miles, the sun is behind us, and it brings out the lovely green of the Prairie; I love the conifers, but to see these massive areas of grain swaying in the breeze was absolutely beautiful.

Frank points to the different sections. "This is wheat" and he named the variety. After a while we entered an area of oats, and so on. The pride on Frank's face was a joy to see; not an arrogant pride, but one of a happy man, well satisfied with his life. We flew for an hour or two. We had not covered the whole area, but we turn for home. "You can see, Jim, why a horse would not do what I need to do on any one day, on the Prairie. Things can need action quickly and this little plane will get me there pronto. Frank glances out the corner of his eye at me, like he is trying to get some idea of my reactions to the day. I don't know what he decided but I felt totally relaxed; whatever concern I had was no more.

Frank had obviously felt the same way about me, as he calmly said, "Take the controls, Jim." Now he had done it again. What? I said, "I don't know the first thing about flying." "I am not going to jump out and leave you, Jim. I just want you to feel the joy of flying. Just take the stick gently, no sudden moves. That's it. You have got it, and we are still flying." And he took Jim through the different control movements. "Okay, Jim. You have flown your first airplane" and he took the control again. "How did it feel?" "It was fantastic, Frank." "I won't ask you to take it down, Jim. That might be several lessons away" and when we were safely on the runway, Frank said, "By the way, Jim. What you missed this morning was Debbie making the sign of the cross on her chest" and he burst out laughing, and as they were safely on the ground, Jim laughed also.

When Frank and Jim walked into the house, Debbie came through with a clean pair of underpants, which she presented to Jim, and the whole house rang with laughter, and Jim felt he ought to score a few points, and so he stood up, walked over to face the family and began to speak. "Contrary to some of the assumptions that have been suggested" with a strong glance at Debbie: another laugh, "I would like to say with pride, that I flew the plane for a while, under the pilot's instructions of course", round of applause, "and I would like to say it was fantastic. Thanks a lot, Frank." "We have an hour before dinner, Jim, and I would like to talk to you about something else. I did not mention it on the plane as I wanted you to do nothing else but enjoy the day. We will have a little walk, Jim, shall we? Debbie tells me that she mentioned to you, while in England, about a little place up the road that you might like to buy. I would like to look at it, and the surrounding area. Would you be quite happy with that?" "Sounds alright, Frank."

"Okay, tomorrow we will do that." Frank sells the idea to the family, and off we go. Just up the road, in Canada of course, was a little different from England, but we got there and it did look quite attractive, though it was somewhat overgrown. It has been eighteen months since Tom and Peggy Roberts moved out

Rosieta and I are looking the house over, but Frank and Debbie are more interested in the grounds. They have even filled a bucket with some soil. They don't say a word, but calmly put it in the Land Rover. "What do you think, Rosieta?" "Well I have to say, Frank, it is very, very isolated, isn't it." "Yes, I would have to agree, it is. But it was well worth a look, wasn't it?" Well all aboard and off we go back home. It had all been a little strange. As soon as we got back home, Frank and Debbie took that soil out into the yard, and with her instruments, Debbie lets out a "yippee", and Frank can hardly control himself, and they look the soil securely away. No more was said, but next day Frank and I had another talk. "Jim", he said. "I would like you to buy that cottage up the road. Don't ask me why, Jim. Please trust me. Come with me to the agent, tell them you are from England and would like to move to Canada with lots of peace and quiet. Will you do that, Jim? When the house is yours, Jim, I will tell you why. You will be happy with the purchase, and if you are not able to accept the situation, I will buy it from you in three months. Do this for me Jim, please." "Okay, Frank. I like you and I trust you."

This morning, Frank and I are on our way to the agent selling that little place up in the road. "Oh just one more thing, Jim. Let me do most of the talking. I know these guys." "Okay, Frank." "And here we are.

You are my brother-in-law from England, and you are looking for some space, with peace and quiet. Hard to find in England. Okay, Jim?" In we go, met with open arms, of course. "Good morning, gentlemen." "Good morning, my name is Frank Ruane. This is my brother-in-law from England. I have told him about the old Roberts' place. Tom and Peggy moved out about eighteen months ago." "Oh yes, sir, I know it now. Lovely little place, so quiet, no trouble." "Well, that is what Jim here is looking for, aren't you Jim?" "Yes, very much so" said Jim. In England, especially where I live, there are so many vehicles and people; and slamming vehicle doors and argumentative people are what I'm hoping to leave behind. I love England, but I am looking ahead."

"I well understand, sir" and he goes on to describe the property and hands up a print-out. It covers a rather large area, but it needs no upkeep and has a great timber potential. It would be a case of doing as much as you wanted, or as little." "You describe it in glowing tone, sir, but now the price. I am not one of Canada's oil magnates." "I do appreciate that" and he named a figure, "and I think because it has been so unoccupied for so long, that we can bring that down too" and he dropped the price quite nicely. "Well that's very good of you, sir, but I still think you are to a high standard." "I have bought you, Jim, a long way to talk with you about a rather rundown, overgrown property. That would, I thought, be in his means. He has little knowledge of real estate, but I have, and I think we will have to leave it, thank you." "Just a minute, sir. Let me ring Mr. Roberts. He might have prepared to accommodate you" and he goes off in the other office. He comes back all smiles and says, "Mr. Roberts is prepared to accept" and he names the revised price. "That's a relief" said Jim. "I like the place, but I have to balance my budget, and Frank her has not prepared me for the asking price."

Everyone was all smiles and when the paperwork was all attended to and the handshakes made; I was the proud owner of Maple Cottage. Outside, Frank shook my hand and congratulated me on my performance, to which I said, "Well, you put on quite a show."

That evening, we all gathered around that large oak table and Frank began to speak. "I told you Jim that when Maple Cottage was yours I would explain why I wanted you to buy it. I myself could not buy it for reasons I will give. You see, Jim, you are now a potential multi-million or billionaire. When Debbie put her Geiger-counter on that bucket of soil, it almost went off the dial. That area around that cottage is intensely radioactive, and the reason is probably that the area is sitting on large deposits of uranium." A quiet cheer went up around the table. They hugged, shook hands, kissed, and cheered. But not Jim. "You have just gained millions, Jim. Not lost it. What is troubling you, Jim? Tell us, Jim.

Chapter Thirteen

Jim, what is troubling you?

"Frank, Frank" said Beatty. "Whatever is troubling Jim is obviously serious to him, and is maybe to us? Please tell us, Jim, what so concerns you. We have as long as you need." "Thank you, Beatty and family. I feel a bit of a rotter, but I cannot join in you excitement while I feel the way I do. Although I do know that Frank has pulled off a wonderful position for the whole family, it may be my name on the deal, bit I see it as the family. When we, Rosieta and I, met you all, we felt a true welcome; a beautiful beaming Debbie with Richard in Winnipeg, a lovely smiling lady with another of those beaming Debbie smiles, who came running out of a lovely house, almost tearing Rosieta apart in a wonderful hug. And in the evening, I saw a man, obviously well-satisfied with his day; Frank look like my kind of guy. Now I come to what concerns me so much, or have you had enough?" "Carry on, Jim" said Frank. "I will" said Jim. "But I want you all to agree to disregard every word I say completely, if you find it just plain foolish, agreed?"

"Okay. While you were justifiably excited, I began to see you all quite differently. First I saw Frank on his beautiful cruiser in the Mediterranean, visiting Cannes, Gibraltar, Toulon, with all his hangers on, drinking his whiskey. And when they had gone to their cabins, Frank was there watching the night sky, thinking what a useless life this was, and thinking back to that guy who ran that great grain empire, feeding Canada and a large part of the world, with a family that had such a great love of him that it really showed. And then I saw Beatty in that very large apartment in the Delta Chelsea hotel, hosting the parties, opening functions over the city, wife of that great financier, Frank Ruane. Could it get any better, she would ask herself, and if you listened carefully you would hear her say, "yes, it could Beatty", in a lovely old house with my family around me; a family who needed me and loved me."

"That lovely daughter, Debbie, had everybody dancing to her tune. She had moved to Ottawa. All the city knew of her. They came to her lavish parties, to dance with Debbie Ruane was every young man's dream, but when the last one had gone, she sat alone with the glass, topped up with champagne and her memories. Tears trickled down those lovely cheeks, and she remembered the man that really loved her. Not these guys who just drank her wine. She would like to forget all of this life and go to him, but she was of that proud Ruane stock; and anyway, would he want her now after all that he must have read and heard on the radio? She could not have known, of course, that had had contacted Richard, he would have immediately been on his way to bring her back to the home she had loved. Richard still lived there, hard as it was when he thought of days gone by."

"The last one I saw in my crystal ball was Richard. The oil magnate who had bought Frank's grain empire; knew nothing about running something of this size, and Frank had asked Richard if he would stay and run it for him. Richard had learnt a lot from Frank, and decided he would go for it, and the men who Frank had treated so well were very keen to help Richard. And so the only one in my crystal ball contented and happy was Richard. He would be even happier if he could get his Debbie back, but in her high society life he thought she would not want to know him anymore."

"Well that's it, dear family. I am sorry that I had to ruin your evening, but let it only be your evening. Do as we agreed, disregard everything I have said. Put it out of your minds; consider it the rantings of a fortune teller – unless you think I could be right. I am going out into the garden to sit on that seat by the roses, and watch a beautiful sunset; a Canadian sunset, as it drops down behind the conifers, in that which I find very difficult to get in England – silence." Jim made his way slowly to the door in absolute silence. The friends and relatives that he had come to love so much were devastated. Several minutes went by before he heard any conversation. When he got to the seat, it now not to look at the sunset, but to bury his head in his hands. He could not believe what had come over him. He had destroyed their dream. He was pleased now to hear a quite heated discussion; at least they will come to a decision that will be to their liking, not mine. His eyes went up to that sunset, quite beautiful until this evening. He had so enjoyed this holiday that the family had asked Rosieta and himself to have with them. Now what would it be like having this prophet of gloom and doom with them? Jim felt like catching the first plane home.

He had watched the sunset; a beautiful sight, but he was not too pleased with himself, and he had dozed off. Now he was being gently shaken by Beatty. "Come on, Jim. You must have fallen asleep." "Oh dear, oh dear. Sorry about that." "No problem, Jim." And when he was completely awake, he could see the rest of the family. They all had a chuckle, and then Frank, who was carrying a tray of wine glasses on it, handed them round. "Now" he said. "I will hand you over to Debbie, who feels that she owes you so much." "Had we gone down our road, I think I would have lost the most, Jim" she said, and she pulls Richard closer to her. "No riches in the world could replace what Richard and I have at this time, with our wedding and a wonderful family, and so much to look forward to. "We all thank you, Jim" and she raises her glass again. "Thank you, Debbie, and thank you all but I did not expect this. I thought you would be carrying a shot-gun, not wine. But I would like to tell you what prompted me to launch into that lecture."

"Without giving you another lecture on religion, I would like to tell you why I think I did get carried away. I had remembered a sentence that I was taught at school all those years ago, and this was it. 'What shall it profit a man if he gain half the world and lose his own soul? Seeing what you all had, it really hit me, and in a roundabout way, I tried to interpret it to the situation I saw before me. The difficulty for me was that I was a guest in your house. What right had I to try and influence your way of life? Well it has all ended happily I think, and now if you are not all ready for bed, I would like to tell you what I think might be a solution to this very pleasant and exciting problem. But let me remind you all, what I say is the opinion of one man, me, and there are six of us here who could be very much affected by the outcome of tonight. What I would like to do is to go back to England, after a wonderful wedding that I would not miss under any circumstances. I can't wait to see that beaming Debbie smile with that confident young man, Richard, with the world at their feet. Where was I? Oh yes. Go back to England and after a day or two, take Rosieta to London to a top grade law firm, give them the details that I will have prepared and ask them to prepare a will from them. Having been notified that the will was ready, I would like to invite you all, with John, Pamela and Ron, to go with me to hear it read out, and for you all to question anything that you thought was not in the best interest of us all. I

I would like to set up a trust fund, where each and every one of us is governed by the other. It would be sown up so tight by that that we would all have complete trust in each other. Any member of the trust would be able to draw cash from the fund with the agreement of the other members, up to an amount that would also be subject to agreement. Well that would be the basis, but you will all have ideas that I would like to take with me to include in the will that I ha to the solicitors. Every idea is important. We must all be happy with the outcome. I would not want to feel that I was responsible for any mess that developed. Now I want to hand the chair to Frank, who after all was responsible for this very happy situation we find ourselves in, and to whom we all, I think, owe a great deal." "Well, Jim. I started the ball rolling, but you have certainly picked it up and run with it, and I am happy to leave it for now where you have dropped it. We will all no doubt think of a few things to discuss with you later. I am very pleased that you will be with us for a week or two yet. Thank you, Jim, from us all." And with gentle applause, a very difficult evening was over. "Thank you all very much. Now the moon has risen. It is a lovely evening and I would like to take my lovely Rosieta for a stroll in your very large garden." He takes a hold of her and they walk out into a beautiful, relaxing evening. Jim felt that he did need to relax. He was sure that inside the discussion would go on, but he himself felt at ease.

When Jim woke next morning, he was still a little uneasy. Had they really forgiven him for what he had said yesterday evening? He soon had his answer when Debbie asked if she could give him another riding lesson. This, he was quick to accept.

Chapter Fourteen

Debbie's wedding day is almost here

"Thank you, Debbie. How do you get up on?" "Richard" she calls. "Can you help Jim up on old Swifty?" "Good gracious, Jim. You are a glutton for punishment, aren't you!" "Richard," Jim said, "when I was asked if I would like to go riding with such a beautiful lady, I could not refuse." Richard laughed. "Rosieta told me about all your blarney" he said. Off we go at a pace that Swifty was known for, but it was just right for me. To look again at the beautiful country and casually chat to Debbie was marvellous. Canada is indeed a lovely country. "Jim" Debbie says. "I shall be a little busy for the next few days. My lovely day is almost here, Mum and Rosieta have taken care of most things, but now my presence is necessary, and so this may be my last chance to get you alone. I want to thank you, Jim." "Whatever for?" he said. "For being such a good sport. You have been the recipient of much of my humour, and you not only laughed at it, but you threw it back at me, and in the process you raised a laugh from the whole family That is the way I have been raised, Jim. To laugh and be happy, but always to respect the person who may be at the centre of my laughing. That was why I was quick to apologise when dad caught me behaving rather disrespectfully before your flight, followed by a quick rebuke from mum. They are indeed such wonderful parents, and I hope my children will have cause to say the same about me."

"From the moment I met you in England, Debbie, it was obvious that you had a good sense of humour. Something that I think a good marriage needs, and when I add that to all that you have, I envy you even more. But try, Debbie, not to change; to always be the woman Richard marries." We plod on at our gentle pace but I am a little startled when I see a bear in a clearing, and it has two cubs playing in a shaft of sunlight. "Do we go on, Debbie?" "Yes, Jim. They won't bother us if we don't bother them. They are really more afraid of us than we are of them. They seldom home near the house, and when they do, any noise and they are gone." We go on for a little further before we turn and go through by the wheat. "Hold it, Debbie. I have this urge. Whenever I stand by a sea of flowing wheat, with the breeze gently moving it from one side to the other, to stop and soak up a wonderful feeling. And with the sun bringing out the colour, it's marvellous." "Yes, Jim. I have been away from it for a while studying in England, but I thought of it a great deal, and if I cannot decide on what to do at some time or other, then this is where I will be." On a little more and Jim says again, "Debbie, I would like to ask you about something else before we go home." "What's on your mind, Jim?" and Jim chuckles. "I always have to laugh when a lady asks me that" he said. "The problem I have is our potential wealth. Don't you think we should have a geological survey done before we do anything else?

Supposing there is another explanation for the radioactivity, and there is no wealth potential?"

"Please, Debbie, don't look upon me as a gloom and doom guy. It is the way I have always been. I have to make sure of a thing before I jump into it, unlike my son who always says it will be alright. If the surgery were to prove positive, I would be as pleased as the rest of us" "I don't see you as a gloom and doom man; quite the opposite. I have enjoyed your sense of humour. What you propose is only common sense, and when welcome back from our honeymoon I shall set the wheels in motion, and we shall do a survey. Okay, Jim?" "That's fine, Debbie. Let's go, Swifty."

We get back to the yard and Debbie calls Richard. "Would you unload Swifty?" "Unload?" says Jim. Richard gently slides me off. "How was it, Jim?" "It was great. I enjoyed it immensely. Scenery, conversation, some silence, and lovely company. I could have asked for more. "And I found him the perfect gentleman" said Debbie. "Well, Jim. I am going to be rather busy for the next few days. There is so much to do. Sometimes I ask myself if it is all worth it, but I know it is, as that lovely song says, 'This is the day I shall remember always'. Mum and Rosieta are leaving no stone unturned to make sure of it. I am so excited with so many visions of the life ahead for Richard and myself, and I am sure we both have the courage and determination to see that this excitement never dies. Well, Jim. That was Beatty's meal bell. She uses a bell to call us, as she knows her voice would not be quite enough."

Over the meal, there were the usual laughs about my riding, and I assured them I enjoyed it and think that Rosieta might like it. But I think I detected a distinct lack of enthusiasm in her reply.

Chapter Fifteen

A lovely unusual wedding

The happy day has arrived. Debbie's wedding day, and the house and garden is now covered in tents and tables, with flowers everywhere, a microphone by the door with small speakers all round, and I am going to lose myself, having given a rough idea to Rosieta as to where I will be. The wedding will take place here at the house. A friend of Frank and Beatty, Pastor John Everett, will conduct the service. It will be quite different to our church marriages in England, but the pastor will make it quite plain that it is not to be entered into lightly.

The time has arrived. The garden is full of happy people chattering away like feeding time at the zoo, and now Pastor John stands by the microphone, which he taps; the noise is picked up by the speakers and silence descends on the gathering. "Good afternoon, ladies and gentlemen. I am Pastor John Everett. I have known Frank and Beatty for many years and I am very pleased to have been asked to perform this ceremony of the marriage of Richard and Debbie. Those of you who are from England might think that we take marriage a little less seriously than you, and our ceremony is a little DIY. But let me assure you, and everybody here, that here in Canada, in this garden, the same commitment is demanded of the bride and groom as it would be if it was taking place in Westminster Abbey. But I do not need to tell Debbie and Richard that. Having me them I can see their commitment is rock solid."

John and Richard have stood by Pastor John while he spoke and now the wedding march begins. Debbie and Dad come thought the house to the doors where Richard and the best man, John, stand. Debbie now stands by Pastor John and Richard steps forward to stand facing her. Hey both have a lovely happy smile; there is absolute commitment on their faces. Pastor John now invites them both to make their pledges to each other. Richard begins, "I give you, Debbie, my love which is more precious that money. All that I have it yours. Nothing shall be withheld. All that I ask is for your love for as long as we both shall live. These things and more I pledge to you this day, for as long as I live."

Debbie speaks, "Your love to me, Richard, is indeed more precious than money and shall be returned with all my heart. I shall make my home with you, full of warmth and happiness in which our children shall know the happiness that we have had. We will travel, Richard, and our children shall know of the lives of other children who are not so fortunate. All I ask, Richard, is that we both remember the vow we make today." And Richard says, "I will remember." Pastor John now speaks, "Richard and Debbie, you have made your promises to each other. I would like you both now to consider. You made them before myself, a man of the church, and as such, you made them before God. Therefore they bear the same solemnity as they would in any church in the land. In your mind, I would ask you to add, till death us do part."

The Pastor is still holding their clasped hands and he asks John for the ring, which is placed on Debbie's finger. He now adds the blessing of the church, and loudly says, "Now you may kiss the bride. I pronounce you man and wife." The bride and groom could not be happier. The ladies and the more important are gathered round. I congratulate Richard and kiss the bride and I now I am heading for a nice quiet place by the fence and a shrub. Here I think, I can sit and meditate. Lovely. This was, I think, the shortest period of meditation on record. Here comes a lady, heading straight for me. She seems to know just where I was. "Hello Jim. Will you do my husband and I the honour of joining us at our table? I am, by the way, Beatty's sister. We would also like to know about England. It is a long time since we were there. "Yes" says Jim. "That would be nice" hoping that Beatty's sister was not a mind-reader. But how could he refuse? There was no way out.

At Beatty's sister's table, she introduces Jim to her husband, Clive, "and my name is Jim." "You have found Auntie Debbie. That's nice. And I expect Uncle Clive wants to know all about you. Have you told him about your writings?" "No, he hasn't. What's this then, Jim? Not some sizzling sex story?" "No it is not, Clive. My story is really aimed at the older folk" and Jim is beginning to suspect a conspiracy here; one of Debbie's. He thinks he just can't leave it there, and so he says that the sexy bits are very mild compared to today's stories. "Well, you can't leave it there, Jim" Debbie says. "No, come on, Jim. How's it go?" and Jim glares at Debbie, who has a wide grin on her face, and he now realises that it has all gone quiet and the rest of the guests have also been listening" "You have done it again, Debbie, haven't you. This table is wired up to the main

microphone, and it was you have lured me to this table."
Debbie is laughing her head off, as are all the guests. "Oh
come on, Jim. Laugh and the world laughs with you"
and they certainly were. "Come on, Jim. Read us a bit
and we might buy the book." Well Jim was now in
between the Devil and the deep blue sea.

"Right" he said. "I will read on, Debbie, but as it
was I am sure your idea to wire up this table, you can
pay the forfeit in the form of a nice big kiss, okay? None
of that peck on the cheek stuff." Perhaps I should not
have challenged her, knowing what she might do. She
took a hold of me, looking me in the eyes, planted her
lips oh mine and hugged me like she would crush me.
She was a big gall. Wow! I was glad to come up for air.
"Will that do, Jim?" she said. "I will answer that when
I recover" said Jim. "That's it, Richard. Where is the
nearest solicitor?" "I would not be too hasty, Richard.
If that is what you have to look forward to, you are the
envy of every man here. Okay, I will read now I have
recovered. Are you sure they are old enough, Debbie?"

"Simmer down, gentlemen. Simmer down. My
book, as I have said, is aimed at the older folk, and you
younger guys may not be impressed, but I think the
ladies of all ages will love it. Before I do, folks, I fell
I must say a few words about this young lady's sense
of humour. I may have seemed a little irate, but I have
enjoyed every moment of it. Rosieta and I have been
guests of Frank and Beatty for a few weeks, and Debbie
has done her best to keep us laughing, though mostly
at my expense. I think the situation that she just loved
and had her in near hysterics was after I returned from
a flight with Frank, and she came running through the
house with a clean pair of underpants. Fortunately, I did

not see what she did before the flight. Frank told me when we returned, and again, I had to laugh.

I have become accustomed to her antics and I shall miss her, but I do hope she can keep her sense of humour through her married life. If she can, then she and Richard will be very happy and I really do wish them all the best; and Rosieta and I hope to see them in England sometime in the future. "Well after that" says Debbie, "I really must reply. What Jim says is true, but I must say he is a great guy. He has always laughed with me. I think the nearest he has come to murdering me was when he found I had rigged the microphone on the table, but he made me pay the forfeit with that kiss. In a way, Rosieta and Jim are in a similar situation as Richard and me. Hey too have had to get to know each other since they set out on this wonderful journey through the autumn of their lives, and by the look of them, it is just lovely. All the best, Jim and Rosieta."

"Now since I have the microphone" and she throws a glance at Him, which with a clenched fist and a grin he acknowledges, "I thank you all for making this such a memorable day for Richard and myself. It has been truly wonderful, and special thanks to mum and dad, and the way they allowed me to run free and laugh, and be the girl I am. They kept the reins on me and gave me a sharp jerk when I was out of order. Thanks, mum and dad. Now I will check on the things we will need for our flight to, now where was it? I have written it down somewhere. Ah well, I will tell you when I return." And with a wave and a laugh she heads for the house. "Well after that, folks, my story will seem a little boring." "Oh, come on Jim. You can't back out now, having whet our appetites."

Chapter Sixteen

The budding author

"Okay, here we go. Shout if you have had enough. Like I said, it is not some sizzling sex novel. It is aimed at the old folk, and their lovely memories that they have gathered over the years. Jim and Rosie are in their seventies, but still very active. They meet at the supermarket trolley park, where Rosie has difficulty removing a trolley and she looks up at Jim and laughs. Jim is not amused. He is in a hurry. Her brolly falls to the ground and she laughs again. Jim is now becoming a little angry, but he too has to laugh.

From that moment, they came together, and decided that they would like to spend the autumn of their lives together, and to celebrate he took her to a little pub called 'The Wheel' at Westwell, in Kent. Jim asked the young waitress for a table in a secluded part of the pub, and the waitress with a grin said, "Not newlyweds". "No", said Jim, "not yet". They had a lovely meal and were not in a hurry to go and the young waitress came over to them. "I hope you will excuse me, sir, but you both look so very happy that I just have to ask you, have you been together long?" and Jim told her the story. The waitress looked enchanted. "Thank you so much, sir." And with a wonderful smile, she returned to the desk and we followed.

As we paid our bill, that smile remained on the waitress. It was as if she would love to see the last page in the book, or perhaps she just wondered how many pages there would be. We both had a hug and a peck, and we left that lovely pub. When we got back home, we just flopped down on the settee and, feeling quite sleepy, when Rosieta sat up and said "Goodness me. I have no night clothes." She was obviously a lady who would do nothing that was the slightest bit outrageous. Jim thought he had the answers when he said, "I have some pyjamas that I never wear. I sleep in my birthday suit." There was a long silence and then she softly said, "Would you mind, Jim, if I slept in my birthday suit?" Jim chuckles. "Rosie," he said, "you still have a lovely figure, curly blonde hair, cheeky blue eyes, and you ask a man a question like that. Any man nine to ninety would love to lie beside you."

She went to the bathroom first and when Jim returned from the bathroom, she was under the sheets and her modesty was protected. Jim now climbed in and they snuggled up together. What a day. Fantastic. Next morning, Jim work first and lay looking at Rosie, wondering if he should pinch himself. Was this really happening? When Rosie work and fixed Jim with an impish grin, but not a word, this brought about a grin on Jim like he had just climbed Everest. Rosie slid out of bed and went to the bathroom, still with that grin, and as she closed the door, she called to Jim, "What is the age of the latest pregnancy in this country, Jim?" Jim could see what she was up to and he said, "I think it is about eighty five, Rosie" and all went quiet. When she came back from the bathroom, he took a firm hold of her, looked her in the eyes and said firmly, "I don't know the age of the latest pregnancy in this country" and they both laughed, and it was plain to see the fairy tale had continued."

"That's your lot, folks. If I read any more I shall not sell any books. Hope you enjoyed it. If not, blame Debbie; it was her idea." Jim received some warm applause and a few more mores, but it was enough, he thought. After a quick search, he found the switch and disconnected the table from the main microphone. He then had an interesting conversation with Clive and Jane, and there were happy conversations all round. It has indeed been a great day. The wine has flowed, the laughter has echoed around the garden, and the day is coming to a close. Beatty and Frank have now joined us. The conversation is mainly close family, though they did bring us into it now and again.

It has of course been very tiring to Rosieta and me, and we have asked our hosts if they will excuse us, and of course they understand how this pair of seventy-plussers could feel. Debbie and Richard are about to leave, with lots of hugs and kisses. The guests are so happy, with the bride and groom literally over the moon and with one almighty cheer and a wave they are gone. Beatty discreetly takes her handy out of her pocket. On top of the temporary loss of Debbie, she will lose her other two guests, Rosieta and I, but that is not for another couple of days and I am sure Rosieta will try and keep Beatty's pecker up and raise a laugh. Frank has offered me another trip in his light aircraft. This time I needed no persuasion, even if bumpy grass runway was exciting. The trip took us over the various types of corn and I really do get a kick out of seeing this mass of wheat, barley, oats etcetera, swaying in the breeze, and I think of all the people that Frank will help to feed.

We head for home and I feel just as confident as I would in a BA airliner, and when Frank says "Come on. You have done it once. Take the controls. Just remember no sudden moves" and I am delighted. It is all for me the thrill of a lifetime. How I wish I was a younger man and could learn to fly. "Okay" says Frank. "I'll take her down. Did you enjoy that?" "It was fantastic, Frank. Something I shall always remember. Debbie's wedding and the holiday you have given us have been marvellous. Rosieta and I will go back to England with some very happy memories. In with these memories will be Beatty's cooking, and Debbie's sense of fun. I may have seemed a little irate at times, but I have enjoyed every minute. When she comes back, Frank, tell her that will you?" "I will, Jim."

Chapter Seventeen

Time to go home

Tonight, Rosieta is making sure she has packed everything and we are both a little sad. We could not have imagined that we could have been received with such genuine pleasure from this very happy family. I think the Canadians are just a very hospitable nation. It is morning and Rosieta and I wonder how we are going to look happy, as Frank and Beatty take us to the nearest train station, but I am sure all four of us will try and keep up as cheerful conversation and of course it is very likely we will doze off.

It is a lovely sunny morning and I shall soak up all I can of the fantastic scenery. We shall, after a while, leave the Corn Belt and be back in the conifers which I also love' and I am glad that Beatty also is able to drive, as it is a long way to the rail depot. I guess Frank and Beatty have thought of all that and with all the bags packed, we just have to have some last minute hugs, which tend to be a little longer. It is obvious we all feel the same. "All aboard" says Frank. And off we go. Rosieta with Beatty, and me with Frank; he is my kind of guy. Conversation is a little difficult since that trolley park and my meeting with Rosieta, and I have to consider myself very lucky. I sure do.

It has been so wonderful, but I can't help now and again, having some nasty thoughts like, we are now a little older, and will carry on getting older. And this will make us a little more vulnerable to all the nasties that seem to come along. But to hell with all that: We are as old as we feel. We will live for today! Conversation was not bad at all. Quite light-hearted, considering what we deep down must all have been thinking, and what did surprise me was that the 'fantastic riches' were not mentioned. I was pleased about that. We were all so very rich in so many ways. It was all around us. Rosieta and I did doze off and so we were gently woken by Beatty. "We are here" she said, and we looked around and it was little more than a level crossing, but it did have a café and we had an hour to wait, so that was where we went. The station was what we in England would call a halt. It served this village and miles around. It was way out in the wild, as is much of Canada; that is what attracts me. A man has room to breathe. Frank and Beatty will spend the night in a little town, about thirty miles back, before facing the very long journey home.

The time in the café went quite quickly. The café owner and the locals wanted to know all about these visitors, and it did lighten our mood considerably. The train is pulling in; the driver will do his best to stop with our carriage close to where we stand, but Canadian trains can be one hundred and forty trucks in length, with three engines, and so it is a bit tricky. It is a strange thought that this very long train with those three massive engines has stopped to pick up just two people. In England, they would say it was uneconomical. Again I think these Canadians have a quite different way of life, and I think they are great.

More crushing hugs, kisses and handshakes. Hankies unashamedly out of pockets, pledges to meet again soon, and we are helped up into the train; quickly heading for an open window where we wave to our wonderful hosts until the train enters a long tunnel through the Rockies. I wrap my arms round Rosieta. I know she will be feeling it more than me, but being a woman and mother, I expect she and Beatty have much the same thoughts.

Rosieta is leaving her youngest son behind. True, he has a wonderful life ahead of him, but he will not be popping in to see her; she will see him even less than mums and dads in England do. Sons and daughters are just too busy, and in Richard's case, that will be even more likely. Beatty is now going to return to a large, rather empty house. During the day she will just see the odd worker in the yard and her dogs and horses. But the farm workers are almost like family and she will get a cheerful hello. Beatty will of course know Debbie and Richard will soon be back and that will help a lot. If, when Debbie returns and has the survey done on Maple Cottage grounds, and there is indeed an underground source of radioactivity, that would be commercially viable, then we will be quickly hearing from Frank. If there is not, it will make very little difference. I am sure Frank and Beatty will come over to England, leaving Richard in charge.

We shall travel all night and in be in Toronto in the morning, and so we still have one more day to look forward to. We still hope to sleep on the train and be ready for our visit to Lorna and Robert at the theatre. All has gone well and we are in Toronto. Taxis are quite plentiful, just like the States, and we are soon at our hotel. Breakfast and a good wash and brush up, and we are ready to hit the town. First stop the theatre. Another taxi and we are there, but it is only mid-morning, and there is not much sign of life at the theatre; and we are informed that the next performance would be at 3pm. We quickly played our trump card and said we were friends of Robert and Lorna, and with a big grin, the guy was off to Robert's office, quickly returning with him. I think the guy was amazed at the enthusiasm shown by Robert for these two visitors. They did not look like VIPs. "Thank you, John" said Robert, and off we went.

Lorna and Robert quickly made us feel at home and whatever they were doing was put on hold. "Whatever are you doing back in Canada? Have you come back here to live?" and we chuckled. "I would not mind at all, but no. We are here for Richard's wedding." Rosieta takes it up, "Yes" she said, "my youngest son Richard has married a Canadian girl that we met in England. The young lady's parents suggested that we come over for a couple of weeks before the wedding for a holiday. The parents of Debbie have a large grain business big enough to need a light aircraft to get round it. Jim was given a viewing by air a couple of time and Frank, Debbie's father, actually let him take the controls. It did, fortunately, have dual controls!"

"Can you fly a plane, Jim?" and Jim laughed. "I have never flown a plane before, but although it was only a small aircraft, just to have my hands on the controls, and the plane was still flying, was just marvellous. If I was a younger man I would start flying lessons right away. I don't know what Rosieta did but Debbie and Frank were happy to show me the grain farm, by air, and from the back of a horse. Debbie knew I had never been on a horse, but she loved a laugh and she had quite a few at my expense."

"Beatty, Debbie's mother, looked after me very well" said Rosieta, "and as we were both mothers, there was much to talk about; especially with all the arrangements for the wedding. It has been quite an experience but we just had to keep a day free to visit our good friends, Lorna and Robert. How are you both?" "We were very well, Rosieta, but after what you have just old us, of what you have done her in Canada, we are green with envy!" "Oh come on, Robert. With this lovely apartment, and lovely Lorna, in this beautiful theatre – What more could you want?" "Believe it or not, Jim, just the wide open country. Well, maybe next summer, but tonight let's all go out for the evening. How about it, Lorna?" "Just give me time to change, Robert. Sounds great."

The theatre tonight has just one of these modern whodunits and I guess Robert knew we would not want to see that, and he was not going to disappoint us. He would take us out to dinner, and dinner in Toronto was something to remember, and here we are. The outside is brilliantly lit-up. It must have its own generation plant. The doorman welcomes us. He obviously knows Lorna and Robert very well. I suspect there might be some free theatre tickets somewhere, and we are shown to our table by the head waiter. The head waiter also seems to know Robert and Lorna well. I think there might be a nice little discount for Robert here. "Thank you, Anton. You know Lorna, of course. This lovely lady is Rosieta Rosalini, and the gentleman is James, and we exchange pleasantries. Anton hesitates, takes Rosieta's hand, kisses it and says, "This is indeed an honour, ma'am" and jokingly says, "Will you be dancing for us, Rosieta?" and with a massive beaming smile and a slight bow, he goes about his business. I think if the music from Swan Lake were played, Rosieta would be on her feet. Fortunately, there was no music – well not of that type.

Robert was well-known in Toronto, and of course whenever somebody stopped for a word, he just had to introduce Rosieta. He loved to see her reaction. I think whatever it costs Robert, he will be quite happy, but I have a feeling that there might be a nice little discount for Robert. Rosieta has met a lot of people here tonight, and she has loved it and so have I, for we may not pass this way again. The building was most impressive. The food could not have been better, and the service was, I am sure, especially to Rosieta, memorable. Nobody kissed my hand but I might have been tempted to throw a punch if they had. I am very much a normal sort of guy.

Robert's taxi has arrived and we are going back to Lorna and Robert's apartment. It is getting quite late, but who cares? We have been wined and dined so we are in a quite happy frame of mind, so the night is young. Back at the apartment, another glass of champagne and we lie back on the settees, and so much of what Rosieta and Lorna did all those years ago came flooding back. Robert was rather quiet. I think he was a little frightened of what the champagne might release from the two ladies, and I am sure the frequent glance of Rosieta from Lorna, and Robert's interest in Rosieta, would result in much pillow talk here tonight. But it had been wonderful. It has been pleasant and intriguing, making a great end to our second visit to Canada. Whatever scenes the memories of our little group may produce, they are water under the bridge. We are, and would remain, good friends, and with the usual hugs and kisses we say good night and head for our hotel. Tomorrow morning will come all too soon.

It is tomorrow and we are in our taxi, heading for the airport. Not much conversation but a great many thought of Canada. What a time we have had, the wedding, the holiday, and to round it off, the lovely evening that was last night. This is indeed a lovely autumn. SO lovely that I worry sometimes that something must go wrong, but I soon dismiss it. After Heathrow, I almost take a liking to Toronto airport. Being much smaller it does not feel so oppressive. The airport workers seem to have more time, the young lady behind the desk even asks me if I would like a window seat; I really do like the Canadians. Perhaps a

Canadian is more relaxed because his country is so big. He feels he has space to breathe. He does not spend his life standing on a commuter train with his nose almost touching another nose. Whatever it is, Maple Cottage seems ever more appealing. Maple Cottage is the one thing that Rosieta and I could, I am sure, never agree on. I could live in the middle of nowhere, but Rosieta I think will always need a town or city around her. She needs people, but I can look after me; although I hope the day never comes when I have only me. Loneliness is so difficult to overcome. I think one never does.

Chapter Eighteen

Toronto airport, farewell Canada

Well we are airborne now and heading over that crowded island we call home. It is indeed crowded, but it is home, and as much as I love Canada, I am still very much British and proud of my British history; any Canadian would feel the same way. Sitting here on the plane I think of all the occasions when I wondered how I would react to boarding a plane. Supposing I got to the departure gate and refused to go on board. What would happen then? I could cause absolute mayhem, ruin the holiday of my friends, all these fears evaporated. It felt no different from boarding a bus. My biggest problem was boredom. Nine hours doing nothing was a long time. A book is very useful. I also think of all the things that Rosieta and I have done' the people that are now our friends, and always will be, having my hands on an aircraft control, riding my first horse, and trotting off through the beautiful conifers. So much we had done that we would never had done if I had refused to fly. Much of what we fear can be overcome if we give it a go, and a new horizon will appear with much confidence and happiness.

The Captain says, "We are a few minutes from landing". Our window seat is great, as we look down on the lights below. It is just getting light but the lights down below are still on. It is light enough to give the promise of a lovely day. One view from our window did amaze me. It was the sight of the aircraft wing and engine rising and falling against the horizon. It seemed as much as ten feet, and yet we felt nothing in the plane; so much we have seen and learned, some of it quite extraordinary, some absolutely beautiful.

Firmly back on the ground now and although I don't mind flying (except for the boredom) it is good to feel the earth beneath my feet, but I hope all who ready my book will feel there is so much outside of our lovely country that flying can give them. It is, of course, true that there are advantages and disadvantages in everything, and the greatest of these is the airport security and the long queue to get through. My bag was thoroughly searched, but of course there was nothing. I did wonder why they picked on me. I didn't think I looked like a terrorist, but the good outweighs the bad.

Formalities over, we are heading home in our courtesy car, which was included in the holiday package. It has been absolutely wonderful, but there is indeed no place like home. Rosie is rather quiet. She is probably thinking of the son she has left behind in Canada. He has a wonderful life ahead of him, so much to plan and do, but he will not be popping into see her. I shall have to try and raise her spirits. I think the first thing is to remind her of that young charmer, Paul. That's bound to raise a smile. Home now and things brighten up as we remember all that we have done, and as we sit there cheek to cheek, Rosie calmly says, "Do you think we will ever do it again, Jim" "Hang on, Rosie. We have only just got home". "I know" she says, "but it is an awful thought that we may be too old." "We will never be too old, Rosie" Jim said.

As Jim thought, Rosie is off to see Sandra and Paul. She must have thought of the charmer but she never mentioned him on the holiday. But she is obviously looking forward to hold him, and while Rosie acts the lovely grandma, Jim is going to relax in the garden. Lovely! Sitting there on the lawn in his deck chair, he just loves the quiet and relaxation. That holiday was fantastic, but this is what he loves; no hustle and bustle, no timetables, no people. Just the birds and bees, and a faint breeze in the trees. On that breeze there is the scent of the roses and that lovely shrub 'Mock Orange'. He really loves to have Rosie beside him, but just now and again, he likes to be alone with his thoughts; I think we all so.

As so often with older folks, that peaceful scene with the bird song gently had Jim asleep. A few shrill bird calls work him but he was happy to drift off again. Rosie is back and she can see him from the kitchen window, fast asleep in the sun. Rosie is a sort of human dynamo, and thinks he might have done a little work, and she is heading his way. Rosie gently shakes him and puts on one of her more stern looks. "Where have you been working Jim? I can't see much of a change!" "Rosie, I have done absolutely nothing. And I have enjoyed every moment. I do hope you have also enjoyed every moment. I do hope you have enjoyed your trip" and they both laugh. "Yes, Jim. I did enjoy it. Young Paul seems to have grown in in that short time, but although it was a happy morning, it has left me with a problem. John was there and he reminded me of something that I must devote a little thought to; my house. I have tried not to think about it, but he convinced me that I must make a decision, now that Richard no longer lives there."

"I do not want to sell it, Jim. That is not because I expect to go back there, but it carries so many memories of days gone by. Taking a load of money for those memories, I just cannot do. Can you understand that, Jim?" "I can understand that, Rosie, and to be honest I have worried occasionally that your lovely house might draw you away from me. But you don't have to sell it. There are other ways to see it does not fall into disrepair. How about short-term letting? You would of course have to make sure that the tenant was of the right type, but this is not so difficult. I have never done it, Rosie, but I believe that you can let it on a short-term basis, say every six months at a time; renewable if you are agreeable, and if you ask a large deposit then you should get a good class tenant."

"Jim, that sounds great. I don't have to sell it" and he gets a hug. "That is a marvellous suggestion. John never mentioned that. He seemed to want me to sell it. I will tell him what you have suggested." "No, don't do that, Rosie. Let him think it was your idea. I would not want him to think that I have influenced you in any way. This is between you, Richard and John. One thing you must do is be sure you have a proper will drawn up." "I would trust you to the ends of this Earth, Rosie, but to avoid any distrust between the boys, that solicitor's will is essential. How about a little relaxation now, Rosie?" and she chuckled. "I was thinking of going out for lunch. What do you think?" "I think that would be just lovely. Anywhere in mind?" "I would like to go back to that little pub, 'The Wheel'." "Oh, that is a marvellous thought. Let's go."

Chapter Nineteen

Nostalgia

On their way to that little pub in Westwell, their thoughts go back to the day their fairy tale began. So much has happened, from a supermarket trolley park, to a very large grain empire in Canada, the wedding of her son, meeting Lorna, her ex-ballet troupe, and so much more, and they were so happy that they believed Ron when he said it will be alright. WE open the door and are met by the young lady waitress. She looks so hard at us but she is not quite sure of her thoughts, and shows us to our table. But strangely enough, it is the table we had when we came here before. Had she recognised us?

The young lady brought our meal. She still had that rather inquisitive expression but just smiled and placed it before us, and it was very nice, obviously cooked on the premises. We sat and chatted. The pub was not too busy yet; it will be soon. Rosieta hate to make things difficult for anyone and again she asks the approaching waitress, "Are we holding you up?" I think that gave the young lady a clue as she immediately began to apologise for her reactions when we came in. "Please accept my apology for the way I started at you when you came in, but you looked just like the couple who came in a few years ago. At that time, I was absolutely entranced by what they planned to di. They must have been in their seventies and they were going to start a new life. I am beginning to think I was right, was I?" "You are quite right, my dear. What you remember is correct. We did indeed start that life and the extraordinary story we told you then has just gone on unfolding into the wonderful life that we enjoy today."

"Remember, my dear, when you get to our age that you are as old as you feel. Never admit defeat, get over that first obstacle and you might go on for miles and miles." "I am so glad you came in. I have thought of you a lot. What you were planning seemed almost impossible, but you did it, and are doing it. I most heartily congratulate you both, and I shall not forget what love and determination can do.

With that, the lady cleared our table and made her way to the desk, and have followed to pay our bill and a little for making our stay so enjoyable. The young lady went to the door and opened it for us. We both had a hug and a peck, and taking our hands, said, I hope your wonderful life continues to unfold, and do please come in again some time."

Rosieta is keen to get the house off her mind and so she phones John to put her suggestion to him. It is obviously not what he wanted to hear. I think he would love to get his share of the cash, but he would know that when Richard was told of his mother's plan, there would be no chance of that. Richard, being the youngest of the family, still had a great affection for his mother, as did Debbie, Richard's wife. "What happened?" said Jim. "Well" Rosie said, "John did not seem too pleased about letting, but he said he would be in touch with Richard and see what he thinks; John did say how he could understand how I feel and wanted to do the best for me. Well that's a load off my mind, Jim. Now I can leave it for the boys to sort out. I have no real interest in the value of the house, but of course, to be brutally honest, I know John has."

Jim also had a load removed from his mind. He will not have to find that solicitor I London to prepare that will. A letter has arrived from Canada. The young couple had a marvellous honeymoon. The destination that Debbie could not remember turned out to be Australia and it seems the Canadians did most definitely speak the same language. Debbie has now had that survey done on Maple Cottage and it seems the fantastic wealth does not exist. The survey results did not rule out the possibility that it could be found somewhere in that fifty acres of conifers, but the area from which Debbie took her sample only applied to a ten metre radius, and the only explanation that the survey team could offer was that it was possibly the result of a meteorite having fallen to Earth some time ago..

They did not think the radioactivity was enough to cause a problem to anybody living in Maple Cottage. Jim was really pleased as he was convinced that the great wealth, that Frank and Debbie thought was in the grounds of Maple Cottage, would only bring unhappiness to the family. The whole family were quite wealthy, or would be eventually. Frank had his great grain empire, and of course John and Richard would one day be the heirs to Rosieta's assets. What they amount to I do not know, neither do I want to; I just hope that Rosieta's will is not read out for many years to come, and of course I may not around to hear it.

I was however surprised at the tone of the letter from Frank. When we were with him and he thought the riches were there, he was almost controlling, but in his letter he just says, "You were right, Jim, and I am very glad that you bought be down to Earth. I have thought of that evening a great deal, Jim, and what you saw in your crystal ball. And much of it would, I think, have turned out the way you saw it, and none of us would have been as happy or content as we are today. My grain empire, as you called it, is still feeding the nation, and the world beyond, and I come home in the evening a contented man to a happy home. Beatty runs the house and yard, the cooking is just the way I like it; not how some hotel chef thinks it ought to be, and to see a happy contented wife with that big grin is all I want. She's great."

"Debbie is becoming a very successful geologist. What she learnt in England, she has put to good use, and the company she works for it well pleased; and because the company is pleased, she is a happy woman, and of course Richard is happy to see her that way. By the way, Jim, she still has that sense of humour! Lastly, Jim, there is Richard. Last but certainly not least. He is my right hand man. I asked him if he would like to join me or find his own way in Canada, and I was so relieved when he said he would like to stay, and be a good as me; and the way he has taken to all that is involved – I think he might be better! I give him a lesson on flying now and again. I was so pleased you tried it, Jim. We do hope to see you in England one day, Jim, but if you and Rosieta would like to come over, well, we would love to have you again. And I am sure Debbie could think of something; perhaps a faster horse!"

Needless to say, when Rosie saw the letter, her imagination took her back immediately. "What do you think Jim? Would you like to go again?" "You know I would, Rosie. How do you fancy Maple Cottage?" "Sorry, Jim. I just could not live in such isolation. I know you could, but not me. I have had so many people around me all of my life, I cannot change now." We left it there. I understood completely. Whenever I think of losing her I am sure that such a situation, dumping her in the middle of thousands of acres of conifers would most surely bring it about. I could live in an apartment in the middle of Toronto if it meant I always had her with me. "We will go back again, Rosie. When I see your enthusiasm, I almost think you are Canadian, but I know how you feel because I feel the same way. But my pride in my British history will always make me say loud and clear, I am British."

I think it is not just Canada; I think it is because her son Richard is there. When she is rather quiet now and again, I think in her mind she is with him. I guess he will always be her baby. It would not be possible for a woman to forget those very early years; the love and affection that she must give that baby would always live in the memory, no matter how old the son or daughter became. And so as a man I am very happy to help her if she becomes a little too emotional. Today she can satisfy her maternal feelings a little, as we are going to visit Sandra and young Paul. I feel a little easier now that she and the other Grandma get on so well. Today I am engulfed in utter despair. Am I to see Rosie die, as Marjorie did? I really don't think I can. Is this the end? What can I say to her? I feel so helpless; Rosie is not well.

Chapter Twenty

Is this the end of our dream?

I had been to see my friend Fred again, and was pleased to see both he and Francis were much happier. But in our home, happiness might be very hard to find, for a very long time, we were both devastated. I opened the door, but could not see Rosie. I called up the stairs, "Where are you, Rosie?" "I am up here, Jim" she said, but there was nothing else. It was completely quiet. Jim felt that something was wrong and quickly made his way up the stairs, and there she was sat on the side of the bed with tears in her eye. "What is wrong, Rosie? What is wrong?" I have been to see the doctor, Jim, about a lump on my breast." "Oh no, Rosie" and he sat down beside her, and she flung her arms around him. "Perhaps it was benign and an operation will take care of it." "I don't think so, Jim. I put that to the doctor and she said it is possible, Rosieta, but I don' think so." "But it might be, Rosie! We still have to see the consultant." "Yes, Jim. It still might be" and she burst into tears again. We sat there with our cheeks together and our tears mingling with each other's. There were no more words, until Jim said almost in a whisper, "Is this the end of our dream, Rosie? How very cruel fate can be."

Rosie then stood up and, looking Jim straight in the eyes said, "No no no, Jim. Not yet! Stand by me, Jim. Give me all the support that you have given me in the past, and I will do the fighting" and she took his hands and raised him from the bed. "You have known me but a few years, Jim, but you know I will not go down without a hell of a fight" and she wrapped her arms around him, and he did likewise. The tears did flow, but the battle lines had been set and Rosie would fight. No surrender ever. I think Rosie was trying to raise my spirits. She could see I was devastated. It seemed that it had hit me more than Rosie, but I knew that she would never let her fear show. As lovely as she was, she was a gal with a hell of a lot of courage. I would have expected no less; she had a great sense of humour and a heart of gold, but I knew that she would fight to the last breathe and if she had to go, she would go down fighting.

I would have liked to have been with her when she went to the doctor, but I was not surprised. She was a woman of great determination and that was one of the qualities I loved about her; support would be appreciated, but fuss she would hate. In little over a week, Rosie had her appointment for the consultant at the hospital. We set off in the car, but it was a very quiet trip. In our minds was the awful thought that the consultant would just confirm what the doctor had said. I felt I sold say something to give her confidence, but what could I say? I waited in the room outside the consultants and Rosie went in. He was a very nice man and he put it to Rosie in the most thoughtful way he could. He had obviously done this many time before, but Rose was sure it did not get any easier for him.

"I'm so sorry Rosieta, but I have to confirm your doctor's diagnosis, and you do unfortunately have breast cancer, but please don't see this as the end. There is so much that can be done these days", and he went on to explain the next procedure. "In two or three weeks, we will start the chemotherapy, and then the radiotherapy will follow after a reasonable interval; and at all times you will be under the supervision of a consultant. Every patient is of utmost importance to us, Rosieta. To lose a patient is, for us, to fail, and that is what we try so very hard here not to do." When Rosie related all this to me, it hit me very hard and I was in tears. I had clung to the hope that it was benign. Now I knew it was not. Awful things went through my mind, like life without her.

Rosie took it on the chin like she always did. As we left the hospital, she had the look of a real fighter, but when we arrived home we were in each other's arms and then the tears flowed freely; but they did not stop her planning that fight for life. In this fight for life, she had all the staff at the hospital: the nurses, doctors, consultants. They gave Rosie and I that feeling that we were not alone. They seemed all to say, "We know what you are going through" and it helped so much. In keeping with that support, we have today a visit from a young lady from the Celia Blakely Unit at the hospital oncology department. She has come to tell Rosie what will happen at the chemotherapy unit.

All through Rosie's illness, I noticed how as serious as the situation was, everyone seemed to want to raise a smile, and they did. This young lady was not exception; she put Rosieta at ease. She has explained that the chemotherapy will lower Rosieta's ability to withstand other illnesses, and that Rosieta must avoid contact with other people as much as she possibly can, even to the extent of being downright rude. "If somebody comes to the door with a lovely box of chocolates," she says, "you must, Rosieta, be a little rude. Take the chocolates, thank the person bringing them, but close the door. You must avoid any other germs wherever possible." This, of course, was completely opposite to Rosieta's lovely nature. Not at all the way she would normally receive a visitor, but we all smiled and understood the seriousness of the situation.

To the young lady, it was just part of her job to put us at ease, raise a smile. So important as smiles would be a little more difficult in the weeks ahead, but we found this attitude in all the staff we met so very important to Rosieta and myself. Rosieta would take all that was necessary. But that smile meant so much.

We were a little disappointed today when a letter came telling Rosieta that she would be under Dr Mittal, and not the gentleman she had come to know. Rosieta need not have been concerned. From that moment they met, it was obvious that Mr Mittal was an extremely knowledgeable lady, and she and Rosieta became just like old friends. Dr Mittal was a lady with a family, and she and Rosieta would find a little time to discuss their families, and I was so pleased to see those grins on both their faces. I have mentioned the word smile several times; a smile is so important. This is what we set out to do. There was still so much to smile about in Rosieta's life. It might have been a forthcoming wedding, a new grandchild due in a few months' time, Christmas, Easter – they were all date to aim for and as they came up, she set herself some more. The fight that she promised me was indeed there in abundance.

This morning, I am in the garden, actually in the bottom greenhouse. I have three and Rosieta says when people comment on the three, that the large one near the house is when I am a little annoyed, the centre one is for when I am a little angry, and the bottom one well away from the house is just for peace and quiet. Well today is just to sit and think. I have not yet come to terms with Rosieta's awful problem. How do I behave? I need to give her all the support I can, but it must not be what Rosie would call fuss. She would hate that. It is a very fine line, and I must tread it very carefully, or I might demoralise her, and that just must not happen. I must try and keep her as happy as I can. "There you are, Jim!" She has found me. "What is it, Rosie? What's up?" "I have just had a call from Winnie, Ern's wife in Aldington. She would like you to go and see her." "What about, Rosie?" "I don't know. She did not say, and I did not like to ask. Move along, Jim, and I will join you, unless you are expecting someone."

She sat down on the seat and I pulled her to me. To see her face light up was marvellous. "Were you working, or just meditating?" "I was just thinking of all the fantastic qualities that my Rosie possesses." "Oh, Jim. How do you do it? How do you come up with these flattering phrases on the spur of the moment?" "This time, Rosie, it was easy because it was true" and he was rewarded with a smacker. "Now, Jim. Getting back to the reason for my visit to your citadel, I would like to ring her back and tell her when she can expect you." "Okay, Rosie. Tell her I will be over this afternoon if that is convenient." "Okay, Jim. I will ring her. Perhaps we can get the prom laid on down to here, Jim." And she went off with a chuckle and Jim was pleased about that.

After dinner, I prepared for my visit to Erne and Win. I was somewhat intrigued as to what it was that I could help them with. "Now are you sure you will be okay, Rosie? It might take all afternoon." "Jim! Jim! When we talked about how we would approach my problem, you agreed that you would give me all your support, but I asked you, while I will need all the support you can give me, that you do not make too much of a fuss of me. I am sorry, Jim, but I cannot stand anyone fussing over me. You must have noticed this." "I have, Rosie. Sorry love." "I will need every bit of help you can give me, Jim, and I know the day will come when I need a little more than support, and when that day comes, Jim, you will not have to ask me. You will know, and I shall feel the flow of confidence that always feel when you are beside me. But Jim, I do not want to think of it. I feel fine and I want us both to continue our dream. There is so much more that we still have time for."

"Rosie, Rosie. Sorry, my love. But you are made of sterner stuff that me. Whoever said that women are the weaker sex did not know you, Rosie, but I will remember how you want it to be. But it will be so hard for me and all those around you" and he wrapped his arms around her, and this of course brought on the tears. Rosie was made of sterner stuff, and she took out her hanky and mopped up his tears and with a lovely smile she said, "Thanks, Jim."

Chapter Twenty One

The Mediator

"Now when are you going to Winnie's?" "Now" said Jim. "Okay. I will be fine. Give win and Ernie my love and say we will see them soon." "Okay, Rosie" and with a wave he was in the car and on his way. Win and Ern's house had a lovely position in Aldington. It was on a hill ilk most of Aldington, and the view covered a large section of Romney Marsh, with its entire sheep etcetera, until it reached the sea. And it had a large garden. This was great, as Erne was a very keen gardener, and won many cups in the shows. I tap the door and Win answers it with her usual beaming smile. "Come in, Jim. Where's Rosie?" "She's not too good today, Win, and she thought she would just rest." "Oh, okay Jim. Take a seat" and I sit down opposite Erne.

"How are you, Jim?" "Not so bad, Erne. How about you?" "Physically I guess I'm fine, but I need something to get my enthusiasm up. The garden is looking decidedly rough." Win brings the tea. As soon as a visitor comes to her house, she makes the tea. Chats go better over a cup of tea. That's the way she sees it. "Well, Win. I am intrigued as to what I can help you with, but if I can I will." "Erne and myself have a little problem that we thought you could solve for us, and we have both agreed that whatever you say, we will abide by, be your answer in favour of either of us." "Okay, Ernie" says Win. "Put our question to Jim,, will you?" "What I would like to know Jim is this. If you had an anniversary coming up, would you celebrate, or just forget it?" "I personally, Ernie, would just lay back and let it all wash over me and hope nobody had noticed." Ernie's face now had a beaming grin, which he was pleased to turn to Win. That was just what he wanted to hear. "But! But because I know Rose would love to have all her family around her at such a time, I would certainly celebrate it. If it happened to be a diamond wedding anniversary, we it might be the last one."

What happened then, I shall always remember. That grin of Ern's face slowly faded, but it reappeared on the face of Win. She looked so happy. I was so pleased. Win seldom won in Ern's house. This time she not only had got what she so much hope for, but the decision had been brought about by a third party; myself. Now surely Ernie must give her that celebration: their 60th wedding anniversary. I could not have been happier for her. She so deserved it. Ernie was a lucky man. Those sixty years had been as happy as any marriage, but UI think now and again, he failed to forget he was not still a sergeant in the RAF, and on one occasion he came to Rose and I, almost in tears, and he said, "I have upset her, Jim." After a cup of tea and a few reassuring words from Rosie, he gave her a hug and shook my hand and went off a changed men. He now knew what he had to do to put thing right.

I also had a cousin, who left the army as a regimental sergeant major, and he too failed to leave that dictatorial manner behind, and his wife also had occasionally to put him right. He was a tall, well-built guy, and she was slim and lovely, and she soon convinced him. And he knew where his bread was buttered! Well it is time to leave Win and Ernie and make my way home. A firm handshake from Ernie and a very firm hug and kiss from Win told me just how very happy this day had been for her. I had wondered if I had upset Ernie, and so I was quite relieved when, as I was about to leave he said, "Oh Jim. Could you say a few words at our celebration?" And of course I said I would love to, and with a wave I was off to Kennington.

When I got home, Rosie quickly asked how did it go, and I told her the whole story with Ernie's disappointment when my reply to his question went against him, and Win was a very happy woman. "Goodness me, Jim. You haven't upset him, have you?" "No, Rosie. Far from it, as he asked me to say a few words at his party, and I happily agreed." I am sure Rosie's concern as to whether I had upset Ernie was really because she thought a great deal of Win. "I am sure, Rosie that they will be just fine, and Ernie will be very pleased how it all goes." Rosie was reassured by that. She would not upset anyone, not even her worst enemy. That's if she had one. She would see nothing wrong in anyone; I was not so forgiving.

Chapter Twenty Two

The Real Fight Begins

How ironic. Yesterday I helped Win and Ernie with their celebration arrangements, and today a letter has arrived reminding Rosie of the awful road ahead that she faces. But I shall be right there with her. The letter informs Rosie that her first chemotherapy will be in two weeks' time. She was pleased and not so pleased; pleased because she could start the fight, and not so pleased because she did not know quite what was involved. But we were both very keen to see things moving; to us both, every day was so important.

We were fortunate, in a way, as it would be done at our William Harvey hospital. It was only about two miles away, but it seemed like ten miles. I could see in Rosie's face so much anxiety. She would be asking herself what was involved, could she stand it? Would she burst into tears? But she need not have worried. That strong determination took her through, but how would I behave? We waited in the waiting room until called and the nurse took us through. The first stop was to weigh Rosie. Each time we came through she would be weighed. Now to see Dr Mittal, the consultant. She must have done this so many times, but again, the consideration shown to the patient was so apparent. The confidence that she gave us was so necessary for Rosie and I. Rosie knew that the treatment that she was about to receive was so important, that whatever the side effects, she must do it.

Wherever we go, we are met by a smile and a welcome. This was routine for these nurses but routine never showed. Each patient was a friend to these lovely people, and into the chemo room we go. There is a line of chairs. They are in twos; one for the patient and one for whoever brought the patient. The nurse settles Rosie into this very comfortable chair with a few remarks to get her chuckling, and a bit of friendly abuse for me, all designed to lift our spirits, and it did. There were two nurses running the room, and at times you would think these two were in the local music hall. But it did the trick. They would insult each other from different ends of the room and the patients just had to augh. Sitting beside Rosie, I could barely bring myself to look, having found a suitable point, the tube was inserted into her hand and the slow process would begin. It had to be slow and would take about two hours.

I tried not to look at Rosie full in the face, in case I embarrassed her, but she didn't bat an eyelid. She took it as if she was saying to herself, "See what you think of that, breast cancer." With the tow nurses, is a lady volunteer. She makes the tea and a thousand other jobs. A lovely lady, again, with an attitude so very necessary in a situation like this. The lady brings Rosie and I a welcome cup of tea and Rosie makes it plain how very much she appreciates it. They have a few reassuring words with each other. This lay is much more refined, much quieter in her speech. But she and the nurses make a fine team.

Some years later we had to go to the hospital and this lady was still there. By now she must have been in her seventies, but she recognised us, and she still had that smile. We did so admire her. She was just a volunteer, but she did so much.

Rosie will have to go to the hospital every four weeks, and of course she would not look forward to it, but all the time she had that same resolve. That determination never left her. The treatment with this intravenous pamidromate which started in July 2004 will take until June of the next year. Twelve treatments in all. Rosie had one thing to be grateful for, and that was because she had very little of the side effects, of which she was warned. Unless of course she just did not tell me! I could not emphasise enough that the way those nurses did their job made it all so much more bearable for Rosie and myself. As serious and unpleasant as it was, they always seemed to find something with which to raise a laugh, and of course every time that Rosie laughed, it made me feel a little easier.

Six weeks after the end of the chemo, Dr Mittal wrote to Rosie to tell her it was not time to start the radiotherapy, of which she will have six sessions, and this will be in Canterbury; and I wondered if my old car would get us there every week but it did. It was okay. Before the radiotherapy can begin, it is necessary to pinpoint the exact spot to which it must be aimed. As usual in Canterbury hospital car park, even though it is a very large car park, it was difficult to find a place. But having done so, we entered the hospital and booked in at the des. We took our seats with the other patients. It is a very busy place.

Rosie is called and of course I remain where I am, but I can hear some of the conversation between the nurses and Rosie. "What is going to happen today is to find and mark the exact spot to receive the radiation." The operatives have been given a chart and a diagram of Rosie's left breast area, and with their very intricate equipment, they have what they believe is the area to receive the treatment. But to be absolutely sure, Dr Mittal is called. The consultant has seen Rosie a number of times and knows just where the radiation will do most good. She is very pleased with the team, and confirms their findings and a very small mark is made on Rosie's breast.

Before they made the mark, they asked her if it would be alright and jokingly said, "I don't suppose you wear many off the shoulder dresses these days, Rosie." I think they probably knew of her life in ballet. "No" said Rosie. "I don't, but I still have them and I can still get into them, but whatever you have to do, go right ahead. This is not going to beat me without one hell of a fight." They all said together, "That's what we like to hear, Rosie." That is all we do today except for another chat with Dr Mittal, outlining what will take place over the next six weeks. Dr Mittal is a lovely person. She has the compassion and love of everyone's mother, with all the knowledge demanded of her as a consultant in this awful area of medicine. Rosie and I have the greatest admiration for her.

A week has gone by and of course Rosie is very much aware of that lump, but confident that the chemo and radiotherapy will shrink it and she will win. That week that has gone by means it is time to go for the first radio treatment and again, that feeling of the unknown. How will she behave? How will it affect the rest of her body? How many of those side effects will materialise?

Next day when I asked her how she felt she said, "Fine" and I really do think she was telling me the truth. The anti-sickness pills she had been given, she did not take. She said she did not need them. Hopefully that is how it will remain and now there is a whole week before the next one, so we will eat drink and be merry; or as merry as we can. Life goes on and Rosie is in the garden, hanging out the washing. I could have done it, but all the time I have to bear in mind her attitude to life. I have to get concern, help, and fuss in the right order. I have to be concerned, she will need my help, but she must not see it as fuss. If she was to see it as fuss it would demoralise her, and she might have less of a will to fight, and that I must not let happen.

I was so pleased that she was in the garden, as I have just had a phone call from John, Rosie's son, and he did not want his mother to know. He said that he had had a letter from Richard, her youngest son in Canada, and Rich had asked him if he thought Rosie would be fit enough to go to Canada, when Debbie has her baby in three months' time. I almost jumped for joy. This is just what she needs. She will be over the moon, and I could not wait to see her face light up. But I was not going to tell her. I wanted her to get a letter from Debbie and Richard inviting her, and hear her excited voice as she told me. "Rosie is feeling fine, John. She still has the energy and strength of a lion. She will be so excited, but I am not going to tell her, John, because I want her to receive Debbie's invitation by letter. I want to hear her excited voice giving me the news."

"Would you thank Richard and Debbie from me and tell them what I have in mind, John? She is about to start her six weeks of radiotherapy, but I am absolutely certain that whatever the outcome of this treatment, she will be on that plane. She still have plenty of fight left yet, and she is going to use it!" "Thank you, Jim. I will answer Richard's letter and tell him what you say, and I am sure they will both be looking forward to their baby, and to see you both." I hoped when Rosie came in from the garden that the excited, happy feeling I had did not show up too much, or she would want to know why. When she came in she was down to earth. She asked me if I could cut the hedge, as the washing hit it when the wind blew. "Yes, ma'am!" I said. "I will do that", and I got a chuckle, and that's all I want.

Off to Canterbury again today. Usual thing – the car park is full and Rosie suggests that now we know the procedure, I might as well stay with the car, and then if I was in somebody's way I could move it, and there would be no parking problem. She was right of course, as I could not go in with her, but I did not like to see her going off to the treatment on her own. But when she came back, that determination was still there, and I felt a little easier.

Each session did not take long of course, as although it did a lot of good, too much could do a great deal of harm. And so while she was gone, I would write in my mind 'Huckleberry Hawn' – the book I was on at that time was my account of mine and my two friends' lives between 1927 to 1948. That was childhood 1939 to 1945 war years and compulsory military service. 'Huckleberry Hawn' was so like 'Huckleberry Finn'. The childhood years were 'dog eat dog' years. Money was short. There was of course no 'family allowance' and producing a family of eight children put some strain on the family income, but it was a happy family; although a fight or two was inevitable, especially as seven of the eight were boys.

I was twelve years old when war was declared. It was so exciting to a boy. He had no idea what would happen in the next six years. The excitement would be less apparent when the bombs began to fall, and the people fell dying. Fortunately my family survived, even though myself and four of my brothers were called up for their military service. Looking back on it, my three years in the army did, as the sergeant major said, make a man of me. I travelled of course, although I could have shot at my corporals and sergeants at times, but I learnt how important rules and regulations were. As we become adults, we have to conform. Society insists that we conform, local authorities, hospitals, banks, mortgage, and so many things that are not available if we youngsters refuse to conform to society's rules. The army taught me this, and I think I became a man who lived according to the rules. My thanks to the army and my instructors, who I could happily have shot at times.

Another not so happy day for Rosieta. We are off to Canterbury for the radiotherapy. Rosie will sit in the little group until she is called. It does not take long and is of course quite free of pain, but it is the sheer formality; it's that feeling that makes it a little traumatic. She comes back to me sitting in the car and gives me a smile. All the time I think she tries to reassure me. She seems to know just how I feel, and I think to myself that is my job. I am supposed to reassure Rosie. Then I remember we were going to fight this together, and we will.

Chapter Twenty Three

Fantastic News! Rosie's face is a glow

I think today Rosie will not give her problem a thought. The postman has just gone by the window and one of the envelopes is pink and I think I saw an unusual stamp. I keep my head down on my paper and Rosie goes to pick up the letters, and with a loud call she says, "Jim, there is one from Canada." "That's great. What does it say?" But it all goes quiet. Rosie has obviously not got to the important piece... She has now! "Jim! Debbie is expecting her baby in a couple of months' time and would like us to go over to see them. Oh Jim, do you think we could? It would be lovely, don't you think?" Jim did his vest to look as excited as Rosie, but the thought of nursing babies with a few 'goo goo goo's' was not really Jim. He liked them when they were about two years old and had a mind of their own, and used it.

I could not say I was excited, but I could not have been more pleased; this was just what Rosie needs. If something like this comes up now and again, it will keep her fight focused on target, and she will win. "Well, Rosie. We have nothing on the calendar at that time and your radiotherapy will be completed by then, so let's go for it." "Oh, Jim!" and I get a hug. "I just can't wait, Jim. I think I might become just a little impatient, but whatever happens, get me on that plane, Jim." "You'll be there, Rosie, I promise you that."

The weeks have gone by and Rosie is having her last treatment at Canterbury. There was a slight problem. It seems that five treatments are what is usual given, but Rosie has to have six, and the consultant confirms this. Dr Mittal now examines Rosie and says that she will see her in a month's time. In the meantime, continue with the Tomoxaphine tablets. "How are you feeling, Rosie? Any sickness?" "Not enough to worry about doctor." "That's great. Now I am going to ask a very great favour of you. What I am going to ask of you Rosieta is entirely up to you. Please say no if you are the slightest bit uneasy, and I shall think none the less of you. As in all walks of life, we all have to learn, and in the medical field it is so much more involved. Here at this oncology unit, we are desperately short of doctors to operate it, and I am quite excited at the moment, as I have five new students. But now for the important question, Rosieta."

"Would you be prepared to be a guinea pig for my students? They can read their books and listen to my lectures, but I would so like them to see and feel the areas of the body that it will be so necessary for those who come after you. Very many patients will be so in need of their knowledge that they have learned from you, and me. I must repeat, Rosieta, please say no if you are at all uneasy about this. I do realise that what I am asking of you is not what most patients of mine would expect, and I would respect your discussion, if it be yes, or no."

Rosieta had listened to what the doctor had said, but was still a little hesitant. It was January and cold, and the thought of five pairs of hands feeling for the lump in her breast did make her think a little. She was a woman who did feel the cold. It was not a pleasant thought, but she knew that all she was benefiting by here at Canterbury today was learned by these methods, and she knew she must say yes. "Sorry for my hesitation, doctor, but I am sure you have put yourself in my position a few times before. I think it if was mid-summer I could see things a little differently, but my answer doctor has to be yes, I will do it. I will do it because I know that much of what I benefit from today came from those who did what you ask of me today. All I ask of you is please turn the heating up!"

Rosieta got a great big hug from Dr Mittal and a thank you, so enthusiastically that you might have thought that the doctor was benefiting personally. But this was for her oncology unit and all the patients that will come to her in the years to come. She was a dedicated woman. "Thank you again, Rosieta. Will next Saturday morning be alright?" Rosieta glanced at me and I said, "If Rosieta says she will be here, then we will be here, doctor." I had always taught my family that what they say they will do, they will do?! And it pleases me immensely that they have not let me down.

The six weeks of radiotherapy had gone by quite quickly and Rose had not felt the sickness that she had been warned of, and she was very happy about that. But not so happy about that guinea pig job, but she had asked herself several times, how could I refuse, and of course with Rosie's conscience, she could not. Today is the day and we are on our way to see the consultant, Dr Mittal, at Canterbury. It is a lovely crisp, frosty morning. If I was going for a nice cross country walk, I would be very pleased, but I am taking Rosie to that guinea pig session and I am not so happy.

It will of course be necessary for Rosie to strip to the waist. She will have the doctor discussing her with these five students. They in turn will be feeling for those lumps, and Rosie, who feels the cold, will be hoping their hands have been warmed. But when I glance out of the corner of my eye, she has that look – I would do it and I will. When we arrived at the hospital, we were met by Dr Mittal, and after a handshake for me, and a firm hug for Rosieta, the doctor said, "I have done as you had suggested, Rosieta. I have the heating turned up and I have asked the students to learn all they can from your most unselfish gesture, but to remember that the lady would be feeling a little chilly."

The doctor found me a place in another room with the usual periodicals, and took Rosieta into the room with the students. She turned and grinned at me and I gave her a grin and a wave, and the doctor said, "I'll look after her, Jim. She will be okay." I suppose it took about half an hour until Dr Mittal brought her back, and I quickly helped Rosie on with her coat. "I don't have to tell you Jim, I am sure, how much I value Rosieta's cooperation here this morning. I can lecture my students and they can read every book, but they now know precisely just what they must look for when faced with their patients in the future. They must miss nothing!" Another hug from the doctor and a handshake for me, and we are on our way home with the heater in the car on maximum. As Rosie related what had happened, she could not help laughing herself; and

I of course was rolled up in laughter. Her friends and family said she deserved a medal after they also had enjoyed a good laugh.

I admired her immensely, after all she was not a well woman, but that was the way she was. Rosie would help anyone, and yet she was so reluctant to accept help. She was so very independent, and that of course, coupled with her determination, was what I loved about her. Arriving home, the first stop was the heater control. I think it will take some time to forget those students; and not just for their good looks! After these hospital visits, Rosie is able to put them out of her thoughts and get back to her family life, and today her thoughts are on that baby in Canada. "Jim" "Yes, Rosie?" "I have an appointment at the hospital and so we can arrange to go to Canada just after that, and that will be in four weeks' time. What do you think?" "That sounds fine, Rosie."

Chapter Twenty Four

Debbie's Baby and Canada again

"I think I will phone, rather than write, then we will know straight away if it will be okay. How does that sound?" "It sound fine, Rosie. Can we afford it?" "Oh shut up, Jim. After half an hour you can pull the plug out!" Off she went into the other room and I knew she was still very much aware of our income, and our outgoings. I knew she would certainly not have half an hour on the phone, but to speak to her son and Debbie would, I know, make her day, and when she reappeared it obviously had. "That's it, Jim. If all goes well, we should be landing in Canada in three weeks' time. John has said he will again take care of the arrangements this side. Are you sure you want to go for it, Jim?" "Of course, Rosie. I shall love it. But a man does not see a baby quite the same way as a woman, but I will race to you the airport. How's that?" I think Rosie had seen a lack of excitement on my face and assumed it was not here, and to be really honest, I think I am getting a little older. She still seems full of life, and it is going to hit me very hard if her health suddenly collapses.

Off to the hospital today for Rosie's appointment. It is at the Harvey hospital and so we only need to go a couple of miles. The doctor is based at Canterbury, but is available here on certain dates. Usual procedure, she must be weighed first, then we are shown to Dr Mittal's room, where we await her arrival. She is a very busy woman. She asks Rosie how she has been since their last meeting in Canterbury, and Rosie mentions some shoulder pain. "Oh" the doctor says, "let's have a look at you" and she takes Rosie behind the curtain. I can of course hear the conversation and the doctor calls to me, "Would Rosieta tell me everything, Jim?" "Not exactly, doctor. It has to be prized out of her." "I was beginning to get that impression, Jim. The

The doctor now sends Rosie for a scan and the result did show a slight enlargement of her problem. The doctor does not hesitate but asks Rosie if she would be prepared to have three more sessions of radiotherapy, to which Rosie readily agrees. When Rosie tells the doctor about the Canadian trip, the doctor's face really lit up. She was so pleased for Rosie. She took Rosie's hands and, looking her straight in the face said, "You deserve it, Rosieta. Go and enjoy it, and we will start when you return. Be sure and take all your medicines with you" and the doctor gives Rosie a big hug and says, "I wish I was coming with you." The doctor shakes my hand and says, "Look after her, Jim." Rosie and the doctor were like old friends.

Rosie had not told me about the shoulder pain, but I am not going to mention it until we return from Canada. She will be well aware of her condition but nobody else will hear a word about it. I do not get involved with the packing for the trip, but I do really have to ask one question. "Are you sure you have all your medicines, Rosie?" "I went to the pharmacy with my prescription a couple of days ago, and I have a month's supply, Jim. This is one occasion when your fussing is welcome, as I know my need is increasing. Thank you, Jim.

That last sentence confirmed what I had been thinking, when Rosie said she knew her need was increasing; she is so reluctant to burden others with her situation that she makes it so difficult for those around her like myself. I feel I should be doing more but I do not know what. I do not want to make her feel worse by fussing around her. She would hate that. Much goes through my mind of course, but UI will not let it show. I will do nothing that might in any way make her fearful of what may come. I know they would not mean to, but the hospice did worry me a little when they invited me to attend their afternoon meetings, where the carers get to know each other with the same problems.

The thought was well-placed, but as I was about to go, I could not help asking myself, if I was Rosie, I would wonder why it had been suggested. But I am sure they have a great deal of experience. I had never been there before, but I was so keen to see what the patients could expect, and I was most impressed. There were lovely grounds and the building had balconies overlooking those lovely gardens. I entered the hospice and was quickly gathered up by the staff. I signed in and took up one of the comfortable chairs. We were arranged in a horseshoe shape, and there were about a dozen of us, with three nurses, very keen to help. We were asked to give a short description of our situations and our names. It was very obvious that some of the carers had extremely difficult situations, with loved ones very seriously ill, and were very grateful for any help the hospice could give.

Now it is my turn. I stood up and began by telling the little group my name and the district where I lived, and I went on to say how impressed I was with the determined approach that the carers had with their enormous difficulties. I don't think they were too impressed, as their reply was "Well, you just have to, don't you" "Yes" I said, "we do. And when my turn comes, I hope I can remember what you have said, and that my wife will get the same loving care. She is not to dependant on me at the moment, but when she is, I shall be ready."

We were reminded of all the help and equipment that the hospice could give, and I was already able to feel a little more confident. In my mind I was a little worried. Would I be able to do what I knew would be required of me? I think I shall need them." One of the nurses took my arm. "Now you will come again, Jim, won't you? We can learn so much from one another." "Yes, I will come again, nurse." I had forgotten her name, but we smiled, and I said, "See you next week. Bye." Suddenly my situation had deteriorated considerably. What I had heard from those carers had me worried. Would I be up to it? And then I remembered the words those carers used, "You just have to, don't you." And I knew them. I would do all that Rosie would need of me. I would respond just as they had.

Today there will be no sad thoughts. We are about to leave for Heathrow. John has been as good as his work, and taken all the worry off of us. I am surprised at the family here to see us off. I hope they are not worried. We are not; we are taking each day as it comes, and

I hope our hugs, kisses and waves convinced them. At Heathrow, we now know the routine. Baggage checks, security and that long walk to gate 46 where the plane will leave for Canada. "You sure you want to go, Rosie?" "Just try and stop me, Jim" and she bubbles over with excitement. That is what I so want to see, that lovely face light up. Each time I see it, I am reassured.

We taxi along the runway. The engines open up and we are in the air. This part of flying I love. It is so exhilarating to feel that thrust of this massive machine, hurtling up into the air. What would Wilbur Wright have thought, I wonder? Now the part I don't like. Seven hours to Toronto. It bores me stiff, but Rosie and I have a book to read. Rosie has 'Pride and Prejudice' and I have my book that I wrote a few years ago. It may seem strange but in my book, 'Huckleberry Hawn', I can relive those years of so long ago; my childhood, war years and military service. It is my childhood that makes me laugh; that mischief, almost criminal. We land at Toronto, and pick up an international flight to Winnipeg, where Richard and Frank welcome us with their usual enthusiasm. The two men have come to get us, as of course, the ladies have now another job – Little Richard.

Of course, as usual we fell asleep on the long journey, but so excited to hear the call, "Come on, we are here. Wake up." We get our usual hugs and handshakes, but I could not help noticing Rosie was handed a little more gently this time. I hope Rosie did not notice it. Into the house, with Debbie's around her, and a rather impatient Rosieta says, "Well, Debbie. Where is the young man?" "I will take you to him, Rosieta, but a little shush because he's asleep." "Okay, Debbie. I know the routine", with a little chuckle. This is what Rosie needs. If only it could happen every week. Rosie stood there with that marvellous smile that a mother or grandmother has when she sees a lovely baby; so grateful that their beautiful baby is healthy and well-formed, and of course Rosie thinks he looks like the father, her son, Richard, with the good looks of his mother, Debbie. Rosieta give Debbie a hug, "He is lovely, Debbie. I am so pleased for you. It is great when you know all has gone well, and I can see you could not be more pleased."

Jim of course is not quite as excited as Rosie, but he takes a hold of Debbie, gives her a peck and says, "Thank you, Debbie. You cannot imagine what you have done for Rosieta today." Rosieta did not hear Jim. She was too busy gazing at her grandson. Over a cup of coffee, Debbie, Beatty and Rosieta are discussing the young fella, sleeping, feeding, etcetera. Frank, Richard and I have their work in mind. The price of grain, the tonnage they expect to harvest. Would the weather hold? So much depends on so many things.

Today, Jim thinks, he will leave the ladies to discuss all the things that babies need; the running of the home, parental duties, and all that kind of thing, and he will do what he has been longing to go – ride old Swifty. Would you ladies mind if I sneaked off on old Swifty around our usual route? I am sure you will have much to talk about." "Oh, Jim!" Rosieta says, "We did not come all this way just to ride a horse." "Oh go on, Jim" says Debbie. "I know how much you enjoy it. Richard will help you up." I expect she would have liked to have come too. "Would you mind if I came too?" said Richard. "I am not too busy at the moment." "No" said Jim, "that would be great."

They went gently through the conifers. Richard let Jim soak up that silence and relax. Richard was well are of the anxiety that Jim must have over his mother, but the inevitable question had to be asked. "How is mother, Jim? I may not have you on your own again and so I have to ask you now, when we are alone." "Until a couple of weeks ago, Richard, I would have said she was fine, because she keeps her problems to herself. But two weeks ago, the doctor asked her that question and Rosieta mentioned the pain in her shoulder. The doctor did not say what it might mean. I think, Richard, it has spread to her shoulder." What I said hit Richard rather hard. But he had to know. "But she looks so well, Jim." "Yes, I know. That is the most difficult thing. She does not tell me and so I find it so difficult to help." "Is there anything Debbie and I can do, Jim?" "Not yet, Richard. Presenting her with such a lovely grandson, and this visit, will have done so much. She was so excited when you letter arrive. It not only made her day, it made mine; just seeing her was so uplifting.

Richard could see what effect his question had had, and let Jim enjoy his relaxation, and they carried on to there the conifers topped and the grain began. Swifty seemed to sense that this was there they would stop, and they looked out as far as the eye could see. The wheat was still swaying, but it was now a golden yellow and soon those monsters, the combine harvesters, would move in. "Well come on, Jim. We had better make our way back. I have enjoyed our trip, Jim, and I do appreciated the way you are looking after mother." "Rosieta, Richard, has done so much for me. She has given me a new lease of life. Her humour, her vitality, and sense of adventure, have been the source of our happiness, and I can never do enough for her now."

Richard takes care of Swifty and we walk into the house. "So you sneaked off too did you, Richard?" said Debbie. "I thought Jim might get lost." "Not very likely, Richard. I think Jim knows that route quite well, and if Jim doesn't, Swifty certainly does." "I enjoyed it as much as Jim. It was great. It is not often I get to move around that leisurely. My wife is usually chasing me." "That will be the day, Richard."

When Frank came home that evening, he said, "All the combines are in position, and we will be rolling in the morning." "Oh dear", said Debbie. "There goes your lovely swaying grain, Jim" and we all chuckled. "How would you like a last look at it from the air, Jim? Come with me tomorrow and I will show you an amazing sight. Something you could never see in England, Jim. I see it every year, but it still leaves me enormously impressed; to me the greatest show on Earth." "Sounds great, Frank. What time do you start?" "Any time, Jim. I am not involved much now. It is all down to the contractors?" "But how do you know if a truckload has gone missing?" That question raised a laugh. "No trouble there, Jim. My manager will be there and each truckload has to have his signature, and at the end of the harvest, I make it very much worth his while to look after my interests and his job!"

After the usual Canadian breakfast, we make our way to Frank's little aircraft. He makes sure I am in properly before climbing aboard himself. Our little plane takes a few minutes to reach its cruising height, and we are soon over the action. Already my lovely scene has changed completely, but it will all be there again next year. My mind leaves that beautiful scene of swaying corn and is replaced by a dozen monsters gobbling up the grain; shooting it out into a truck alongside, straw flying out the back, clouds of dust with a very loud noise, heard here once a year.

The grain will go into Frank's storage hoppers, or straight to the rail depot, where much of it will begin its journey around the world, but of course feeding Canada comes first. "Well, Jim. What do you think? A little different from Kent, is it?" "Just a little, Frank. One combine is usually enough for us." "They will go on day and night until it is all safely harvested. Millions depend on the Canadian grain belt, mainly Alberta, Sebastian and Manitoba, for their lives. For me it is a profitable business, but for so many people it is life or death. I am not at all unaware of this, but I do not do this just for the Canadian dollar. I do it because I love it, and know so many people depend on me. Can you believe me, Jim? I hope so. There is so much more in life than just wealth."

"I believe you, Frank, because the man you describe is the man I first saw on my first visit to Canada; a man well satisfied with his day. A contented man with a lovely family." "Thank you, Jim. Now I am going to take a wide sweep around these combines to show you just what an enormous job they have. But they will do it, Jim. It has to be done. It must all be in before the snow arrives; the snow shuts the whole thing down. That's our life, /Jim. We have long, hot summers. The sun gives us ripe, hard, moisture-free grain. That bread bakers prefer, but we cannot ignore Canada's weather. We must work strictly to its timetable or we are in trouble. Now I am going to land on that grass strip over there; I want a word with my manager. You stay in the plane, Jim. It won't take long."

Airborne again, and heading home, "That's it, Jim. What did you think?" "It was all absolutely fantastic, Frank. You have a wonderful satisfying life, but do you think you can turn Richard into a Frank mark two?" "No bother there, Jim. Richard is more of a Frank than me. He puts in 110% and of course he has one advantage over me; his knowledge of business in general that he learnt at university is very useful. He has shown me many ways I can improve." Jim did a slight chuckle. "Why is that, Jim?" "Well, Frank. Just between you and me, I will tell you. While having one of my riding lessons, Debbie said to me, "One thing worries me, Jim. Will dad expect the 110% from Richard that he himself puts in?" I said I didn't think so. Frank knows how hard he drives himself."" "I have never shown any expectation of that, Jim. I have let him go his own way, at a speed that suited him. You see, Jim. He is not just working for me. He is working for his family, and he will do 150% for them. I see in Richard how it was with me. Debbie could not have chosen a better husband or father of her children. Let's go home, Jim." "Thank you, Frank, but don't forget that was off the record. I won't forget, Jim."

Home now and Beatty says, "How did it go, Jim?" "It was absolutely fantastic. To see it all from the air put a completely different perspective on things. It was of course a little sad to see that beautiful wheat cut to stubble, but it did show me just how much goes into making my bread. I seem to remember the last time I flew with Frank. As I entered the house I was presented with a clean pair of underpants. I guess it is nappies now, Debbie, eh?" Well I got a laugh, but not quite so heartily. After dinner, Rosieta asks the family if they would excuse her as she would like to go and rest on her bed. Beatty is quick to take a hold of her, and Jim prepares her medicine. It works very quickly and Rosieta is soon asleep.

Jim now decides that he will have a word with the family. "How is she?" asks Beatty. "She is asleep now. Her medicine works very quickly. It is such a relief for me to know that she has something to keep her comfortable. She never complains but I know at times she needs it. Rosieta does not know what I am about to ask you, and I would prefer that you do not tell her" said Jim. She has so loved her stay with you all, that I am sure you could not fail to have noticed. But now I think she should go home to her doctor, and the radiotherapy that the doctor suggested. Do you think I am right, or am I being over-anxious?"

"You are quite right" said Beatty. "You are closest to her. When do you think, Jim?" "I thought the day after tomorrow. I would like to put it to her very carefully, but I am sure she will agree. She is not quite so well as when we arrived, but to be with you all and to see that lovely baby has, I am sure, given Rosieta a lovely memory to keep as long as she can. Could you then make arrangements with the airline and take us to the rail depot, so that we could fly out of Toronto on the day of your booking?" "Either myself or Richard will drive you there," said Frank "with Beatty as co-driver. Will that be okay, Beatty?" "Yes, that will be okay. Would you be alright, Debbie?" "Quite alright. Just take care of Rosieta", and she takes his arm.

Time to leave our house on the Prairie. This time I really do think it will be our last time. There are a lot of tears and hankies, with great hugs, kisses and handshake, and we are on our way home. In the car, I felt quite a rotter. Rosieta was her old self, happy and chatty, but I had seen it a few times before; it was difficult to know quite what I should do, but Rosieta knows that she only has to shout Jim and I will be there. She would feel in a bad way one day, and really need her medicine, and the next day I would feel I was fussing as she would say, but I think we have done the right thing. I really would like Rosie to have that extra radiotherapy.

At the rail depot, I think it was Richard who was feeling the worst. He was, I think, wondering if he would see his mother again; and if he did, it would not be on this side of the Atlantic. More hugs and kisses, and we are on the train, waving like there was no tomorrow. Rosie stays by that window until she can see the family no more. She sits down and takes my hand, but I expect it was Richard, her son, she was thinking of. The passage through Toronto airport went well and we are on the plane, still holding my hand she falls asleep and that's great. I hope she stays that way; she is really exhausted.

Chapter Twenty Five

A lovely holiday but reality returns

I am impatient to get home, where I have all that Rosie needs, and the last thing I would have expected has occurred; the long security queue has been too much and Rosie has collapsed. I shout for help, "Medics, please!" I was frantic, and to be absolutely fair, the airport first aid group were with me in minutes; there was no delay. In the first aid room, I explained what had happened, and her condition which had probably brought it on. Knowing this, they gave her a preparation to bring her round, and the sight I shall always remember was to see those eyes open again and of course her usual smile. Rosie said she felt fine now, but she was not allowed to leave. We had a cup of tea and a chat, and all the time I had the impression they were assessing her condition and then they said, "Okay, Rosieta. You can go now, and don't do that again" and Rosieta laughed, knowing that what they were doing was lifting her spirits; they were great guys and dolls.

We had a great little holiday. We had seen Rosie's precious grandson and were well satisfied, but I was so pleased to get home to where I really could look after Rosie. As I have said, she would not always tell me how she was feeling. I needed to know. As she stepped out of the car, she looked fine. It was difficult to believe she had a problem. Rest obviously plays an important part. Most of her conversation was of her new grandson, and even I would have to say he has picked up some good looks along the way.

Back to Earth today, we have to go to the hospital for this top-up radiotherapy. Usual thing, first Rosie must be weighed, a blood test, and then the first of three radiotherapy sessions. It is strange that the side effects do not seem to happen, unless Rosie does not tell me. We were happy to get the first one out of the way, but not happy with what was about to occur. No sooner had we arrived home than the phone rang, and it was the local hospital. Our hospital, the William Harvey, had made an emergency appointment with the Canterbury hospital to receive us as soon as we had arrived. We were told that Rosie's blood count was so low that it was unlikely that she could remain standing much longer; she must get to Canterbury as soon as possible. "Can you get her there, or do you require an ambulance?" "I can get her there, and I am on my way." It would be a hair-raising ride for Rosie, but she always says, "I don't drive myself so I must leave it to you!" Well we made it and in we go.

Having found the right department, we present ourselves at the desk. Rosie is quickly taken from me, and I am told to sit over there. Having sat there for an hour, I decided to ask at the desk what is happening; they do appear to be very busy, on the point of chaos, but I do eventually get through and I am told in a rather polite, rather hurried way, that there was a problem finding a bed for Rosieta. But she has a bed, and is receiving a unit of blood. I thought I might squeeze in another question, and I asked, "When will she be coming home?" Again in rapid fire I was told that Rosieta would probably require two more units of blood and it would be a couple of days before she could be discharged. I would be informed!

I thought I would not push my luck and I made my way to the car. The desk staff were a little abrupt, but working in that chaotic situation, it was not difficult to see why. I had the feeling that the whole hospital needed bulldozing and rebuilding to make it possible to work there; but I was thankful that Rosieta was receiving that blood.

The hospital rang me as they said they would, and I can go and get Rosie. I went to the desk and Rosie was produced, and what a difference. She looked full of life with lovely rosy cheeks, and a beaming smile. I wrapped my arms around her, with a kiss, and with a thank you to the staff, we made our way home, so grateful to the staff at Ashford for discovering the problem.

On our next visit to the Celia Blakely unit at the Harvey hospital, the doctor makes a point of telling Rosie just how close she had been to collapse with such a low blood count, and to try and avoid such a situation again. She was arranging for the nurse to come in and give Rosie and injection once a month. Rosie does not bat an eyelid. She has had so many. Because of the type of woman she was, Rosie asked about the cost of each injection, but Ron, our son, quickly said, "Never mind that, mum. My tax will cover that. Accept it gratefully, mum. It might be the answer." The blood count held up, but it was obvious things were not going to improve a great deal, and I remembered Rosie's words when she said, "When I need a little more than your usual support, you will not need to ask me, Jim."

On my next visit to the hospice, we each give an account of what was happening at home, and I have to say Rosieta is not so good, and I outline what has taken place. The staff of course are quick to tell me what was available in the way of equipment, but in my appreciation I put it to the staff that what I would like would be somebody to come to my home and put it to Rosieta. "That will be done, Jim" was the immediate reply and it was. But Rosieta rallied again. By this time it was a little unfortunate, as it presented Rosieta with a problem. Rosie had just received a letter from Phyllis, her sister. There were plans to close the home. The authorities were saying it was not economical to keep open.

Phyllis was asking Rosie if she could come to the meeting and say a few words, and as ill as Rosie was, she felt that she must go. I felt that I should try and talk her out of it, but I just could not do it; as usual, Rosie would give all the help she could, but she would ask for none. It was possible of course that Rosie was thinking of her sister, that changed woman, and was most anxious not to see her slip back to where she was. At the home, we were met by the dignitaries, after which we took our places on the committee table with the guy from the county council.

Angela, the matron, introduced the committee, and the guy from the council opened the debate. He was met by a stony silence. He just spoke of cash, but that was not how the rest of the room saw it. To them, it was about help and compassion, love and understanding; all of which the patients needed so much. To move them and spread them around the country would be devastating. To try and show this, Angela calls on the beautiful ballet dancer of a few years ago, Rosieta Rosalini. Rosie stands, but immediately falls back into her seat, and there is a gasp from the audience, and Angela comes to her side. "Would you like to come to my study Rosieta?" "No thank you, Angela. It will pass. Could you stand in for me James?" "Of course, Rosieta. Just take it easy."

I stand up and try to look relaxed. "Thank you, ladies and gentlemen. Rosieta has not been well for a while, but she did so want to show her support for this lovely home and to show the gentleman from the council how very much we need it, and to convince him of the plight of the patients here, if his council carried out their suggestions. I think the best way I can do this is to tell you what happened when I visited the house a while ago" and Rosie squeezed his hand. On this occasion, Angela welcomed Rosieta and asked me if I would have a few words with the patients. It was a classic case of being unaccustomed as I am to public speaking, but I had a go. The patients were early stage Alzheimer's, women and one man. They were in a very sad stage of their illness; they were losing their ability to manage their homes, but they could still remember them."

"The first two ladies were no trouble, but the next patient was a gentleman who considered himself French, and as I knew this I greeted him with 'Bonjour, monsieur. Parlez-vous Anglais?' But his French was worse than mine, and he launched into the French national anthem; and I joined him punching the air in defiance, shouting "We will fight and we will win" and at the end, a loud and clear, "Vive la France". I sat him down and whispered, "Vive la France". I said to the next lady, "You must be Joan of Arc. "Non non non, I am Marie Antoinette, and I am Madame Lafayette. Ah, oui oui of course". "

"The next two ladies could not speak for laughing, but eventually the blurted out, "We are from Bermondsey!" and I joined them in their laughter, and said it was good to be back in England, and London. I was a little saddened when the next lady said, "I am from Tenterden." "A lovely area" I said. "Yes", she said. "Do you know when I will be going home?" "No, I am sorry, my dear. You will have to ask the matron that." "Yes, of course, dear" she said. Angela asked what all the singing was about, and I told her it was Pierre. For a few minutes he had been a real man again, a fighting man, a legionnaire. And he had been happy. Ponder on this, sir – when you report back to the council, think really hard before you record your vote. These people are very happy here. Let them stay happy, as they drift off into their inevitable oblivion. To me, this is an awful thought; I hope it is to you, sir. Thank you ladies and gentlemen."

I think now Rosieta and I had better be going home, and Rosie stands and I have my arm tightly around her. We get some loud applause. Angela thanks Rosieta and Jim, while looking toward the audience. She then takes Rosieta's other arm as we go the car. "I can't thank you enough, Rosieta, and you, Jim, for making such an exhausting effort to be her tonight." "I am sorry I could not have done more", said Rosie "but I think Jim saved the day." "He did indeed", said Angela. "Now go home and rest, Rosieta, and thank you again so very much".

It is now becoming very clear that Rosieta will continue to get worse, and to help us the hospice have arranged for two ladies to come in morning and evening, and we do appreciate it. They are not only physically helpful, but they really do try and raise Rosie's spirits. But sadly we have this morning had an accident, and we are devastated. Rosie has had a fall, and has had to go to hospital where it is decided that her leg is fractured. It has hit her very hard. Rosie just does not have much energy left, and we are told that she may not last the night. Ron and I sat with her all night and Rosie opened her eyes with a very faint smile. She was not going that easy.

We decided we would go and get some breakfast. When I got to my car, there was a parking ticket on it. I must pay £8.50; I could have wept. Rosie was now dangerously ill, and we had to realise that she could die in the hospital in all that noise and congestion, and we did not want that. If her time had really come, then we had to try and get her a little peace and quiet, and she would have it. I don't want to belittle the wonderful work that our William Harvey hospital does; it has a first rate record, but it is very busy, overworked and understaffed. This of course results in stress and noise. Ron has been doing his utmost to get Rosie into our local hospice. The injury has presented a problem, but we are so very pleased. Rosie can go into the Willesborough hospice.

My visits to the hospice meetings have convinced me that Rosie will be given that same loving care that I had witnessed so freely given. The staff will raise a laugh, have time for the patients, there will be peace and quiet, a balcony to sit and look at the grounds and animals. I cannot alter the inevitable, but I can be so pleased that Rosie is in a wonderful caring place. I will go in morning and evening. In the morning we join in the banter of the nurses and raise that wonderful laugh, and in the evening it is just a chat and to do anything that Rosie would like. It might be something that she did not want to bother the nurses with.

Today when I went in, the lady in the bed opposite had something to tell me. "If I were you" she said "I would have a talk with your wife. She went off out that door in the middle of the night and I did not see her come back." "I will" I said, "thank you". The lady unfortunately was losing her mind and would come up with little stories. When I told Rosie, she chuckled and said, "If only, Jim. If only. What I would give just for a chance to do just that." And she took my hand with that memory producing all kinds of pictures.

The next day, Rosie was moved into a room on her own. I thought how quiet it was. How dignified. But now, when I look back on it, I realise why; it was the one thing I would criticise the hospice for. I think they knew but did not tell me how close Rosie was to the end, whether Rosie did or not I shall never know, but she did ask me to take some clothing in for her. I took it in when I went the next day, and I held it up, but all I got was a flicker of the eyelids; but I took it to mean yes they will do. I later learned that flicker of the eyelids was one of the last things they can do. But I sat holding her hand until I noticed even the very slight pressure had gone, and I went to the desk opposite and asked the lady to come and look at Rosie.

The nurse did a few checks and then turned to me, placed her hand on my head and said, "I am sorry, Jim, but Rosie has gone" and the tears flowed. "Now stay here as long as you like, Jim. Nobody will bother you." "Thank you, nurse. Will you do one more thing? Would you phone my son and daughter?" "Of course, Jim". Ron came in, took Rosie's hand and have her a lovely kiss, and after about ten minutes he said, "I will be going now, Dad. I want to remember her as she was." I had a feeling tears were near. Pam came in soon after and we had a hug and I kissed her, as we looked down at Rosie, so peaceful now. She had put up a great fight, but I knew Rosie would not give in easily. It was one of the qualities I always admired in her; Rosie had one hell of a store of courage and determination. As I came out, I met the padre and he recognised me. We had met several times when he came round the wards. "So sorry to hear of Rosieta's passing, Jim" and he could see I was near to tears. "Come over here, Jim, and we will have a little chat."

He was very good. He told me what would happen now. "Rosieta will go to a little room over there. She will be the only one in the room and you can come and see here whenever you would like. You will not be disturbed; she will be there for three days, Jim. Do come along, Jim, and share those three days with her. Nobody will mind how often or how long. Now I must be going, Jim. Have you eaten?" "No" I said, and off he went and when he came back, he said, "Now don't you go, Jim. Stay here and a lady will bring you a nice dinner." A lady did bring me a lovely dinner, with a dessert to follow. It not only filled my stomach, but it did a great deal for my mind. The chat with the padre an all the lovely people that worked in the hospice did so much to help me come to terms with my awful loss. I could not thank them enough.

Ron took care of all the arrangements, one of which was to have Rosie dressed in her favourite red costume, and on my third visit to see her, she was in this costume, and she looked so lovely. I leaned forward and kissed her on the forehead; it would be the last time I would be close to her. We had occasionally talked of the music we would like when it was our time to go, and one of the pieces was Schubert's 'Ava Maria', and at her funeral it rang through the building. The female singer had a beautiful voice and those high notes could have been heard in heaven. Rosieta loved 'Ava Maria' and I imagined her singing it herself.

The family and friends gathered at the hotel down the road and again they did their best to lift my spirits. At these gatherings in years gone by, I had often wondered how can they laugh and be so happy, but today I realised it is not only to mourn; it is a time to celebrate the life of the departed, the wonderful lady she was, what she had done in life, how she behaved towards her friends and family. And with that sense of humour, I can hear her say, "Eat, drink and be better, for tomorrow, who knows?"

When Rosie had her diagnosis, I felt I would lose her in months. In fact it was several years, wonderful years, and as Rosie said, "Look at is this way, Jim. Every one is a bonus" and she made every one count.

Chapter Twenty Six

Now I am alone

Time, that great healer, had not yet done its work, and I had in no way filled the gap in my life; it seemed impossible. I would never fill it, but I thought of a way that might help. I would take a cruise. In my cabin, I can lock myself away or I can talk to seven or eight hundred passengers on the ship. We travelled around the Mediterranean, calling at Spain, France, Portugal and Gibraltar. The food was fine; the passengers were all nice people. I chatted with many of them. One couple loved a mile from me in Kennington. A girl from Glasgow, a lady from Wiltshire, even had a verbal battle with two Yorkshire ladies, but when I came ashore at Dover, I was still on my lonesome. I think I have come to the end of the road, I tell myself. I can't go on. But a voice within me says, "You can, and you will!" Perhaps it was Rosie.

The problem is everything I see and touch has a connection with Rosie; a pair of sheets beautifully ironed her dressing chest with her hand mirror etcetera, even a preserving pan. Day to day things and every one tears the heart out of me. Some of it is my fault, like the red quilted coat she always wore in the garden. But that is a memory that I love to keep; it still hangs in the wardrobe. As I sit here in the garden, I am suddenly filled with a feeling that there might yet be light at the end of the tunnel. I feel a source of energy. I have remembered that when the family from Canada were over here for Rosie's funeral, Richard said to me, "When you feel you can, Jim, we would all like you to come and stay with us. It will help you to unwind." It would, it would. I will phone Richard tomorrow. This might be the answer. I can have all my lovely memories of Rosie without all those day to day things that tear me to pieces.

I wondered what Pam and Ron would say. I was getting on in years, and I was planning quite a big step, but I need not have worried. They were of the same mind as me. "Do it, Dad. It will help you so much, and we will look after the house." I feel so relieved already. Ron has arranged everything and he will take me to Heathrow tomorrow. I thought he looked a little uneasy. It was a big step for a guy of my age, but I think his motto kicked in, and she said, "It will be alright."

Chapter Twenty Seven

Canada. You coming, Rosie?

With a firm handshake and a hug from Ron, I am taking that long walk to the departure gate for Canada. It was a long walk. Somebody should have been with me, but she was not, and I think of our trips to Canada, and all her light-hearted banter, and her boundless energy. I shall miss you, Rosie.

The boredom on the flight bothers me less on this trip. I had something on my mind of far greater concern. The usual routine in Canada; Richard and Debbie picked me up and took me home t that lovely old house on the Prairie, a great welcome from Beatty. Frank will not be home until evening. The house that Frank persuaded me to buy up the road, maple Cottage, was now going to be very useful. I am going to spend a few weeks up there myself, if I can get Frank to take me.

When Frank persuaded me to buy it, he had thought it was sitting on a uranium deposit, and we would all be billionaires, but a survey has that radioactivity unexplained. It won't affect me. Frank had kept it lived in with holiday lets, and he said, "When I run you both up there tomorrow, I think you will love it." "Both?" said Jim. "Yes", Frank said. "I have got you a friend. Yes, here he comes" and into the room came a very large Newfoundlander dog. "Good grief. Is he friendly?" said Jim. "He would not hurt a fly" said Frank, "not unless you told him to. Just one thing, Jim. He takes up a rather large part of the bed, but he is an excellent blanket."

The cottage was, to me, lovely. I know that Rosie could not have lived in such solation. She had been so much involved with people, but I am so looking forward to trying it. The cottage had one of those large freezers that the Americans and Canadians always have, and it was full to the door, and so I shall not be going shopping. After much laughing and chatting, mainly at the thought of a man from crowded England being prepared to live in such isolation, the family were ready to leave. "You coming back to us, Jim, or are you ready for the great outdoors?" "As much as I enjoy being with you all, I really do want to give it a try. You can't imagine how I could feel. This freedom; fresh clean air, with the memories I have, and with my friend, Bruno. I think I will love it, but I am glad you are all just down the road" and with some great hugs and a reminder to give them a ring if I was in trouble, they are gone.

The thought of silence when I was at home in Kent seemed like heaven, but when I look out of the window here at that sea of conifers, it does seem a little over-powering. But I am sure going to give it a go. The fridge supplied a good breakfast. Bruno is sniffing the air and off we go. It was indeed a wonderful feeling; that lovely clean air almost like perfume, the silence, except for the breeze in the trees, strange calls from birds and animals, that complete freedom, and my friend, Bruno; just one thing missing: Rosieta. But I have some wonderful memories, and a beautiful picture.

Complete relaxation. I am really beginning to unwind. I am asking myself, "Shall I stay here, or shall I go back to England?" The cottage's mine, so I have no problem there, but a nasty thought hits me. What about the Canadian winter? It might be England! That problem could be some way off. I have been invited by the family to join them for a few days, and although I am very happy here, I am looking forward to joining them. I might get a stroll with Old Swifty.

Back at the family house, they were all very interested in how I was feeling after my life in isolation, and I said, "Marvellous" and I thank Frank and Debbie for persuading me to buy the cottage and have my own little piece of Canada. Next day, Jim asked Debbie if he could take Swifty for a stroll. She was a little hesitant, "Only if you promise to keep to the track and you will not go into the forest. What do you think, Mum?" "Only if he does what you say, Debbie." "I promise to keep on the track, okay." Debbie saddles Swifty and helps me up. I can almost do it myself now. "Don't forget, Jim. Keep to the track." "I won't forget Debbie."

I was quite comfy on old Swifty now and I think he too enjoys it. Maybe nobody else rides him. He certainly seems to know the route. Bruno, I think, knew where he would be most furs and snacks.

Jim went off a happy man, but the ladies are very worried. "He has not returned and it is almost evening. The inevitable question will be asked – why did you let him go?! Frank and Richard have arrived and of course the first question was, "Where is Jim?" and as soon as the answer came, it was, "Right, saddle the horses. We must find him before dark." They went slowly along the track, looking for any clue, but there was none. "Surely he would not have gone into the forest would he, Debbie?" "No, Dad. He assured me he would not. He would keep to the track." They were very worried. They had found nothing and were coming to the end of the track. They had left the conifers and were now moving along the wheat, and there he was, in his favourite spot still sitting on Old Swifty, but his body was slumped forward with his arms around the horse's neck. Debbie lets out a stifled scream, Richard takes hold of her. "We must not frighten Swifty, Debbie. Are you alright now?" "Yes" she said, "I am okay, I think."

Frank will walk one side of Swifty and I shall be on the other, and we will walk Jim back to the house. Can you bring the horses, Debbie?" "Yes, I can do that" she said, with her tears beginning, and Richard gives her a reassuring hug. They plodded on to the house and as they approached, Beatty saw the situation, and she had to have a little scream, and she said, "Is he?" "Yes" said Frank. Now I want you to see there is nothing in the way, and we will bring Jim in and lay him on the bed." They stood and looked at the man they had known for just a few years, but they all had come to love him; he was their adopted granddad.

They closed the door and went into the kitchen and sat around the table. "Has anyone still got an appetite?" said Beatty. "Not like I had" said Frank, "but we had better have something." The meal was put before them, but there was no great rush to eat. The men did manage theirs, but the ladies could not. "You will have to excuse me" said Debbie, "I must go out for a little air." Richard sensed the situation and went with her. It was an awful situation. Jim had died in a country many miles from his family, and Frank will have the unfortunate job of informing Ron and Pam in England. That left Beatty and Frank by the table, and Beatty took Frank's hand and gave it a squeeze. She knew this was going to be a very difficult situation for Frank to sort out. "I wonder what time it is in England" said Frank. "I must ring Ron and Pam." "There is a chart by the phone" said Beatty. "Yes there is, of course." "What will you say, Frank? Have you any ideas?" "Yes, I have thought about it. I must. This is a very big problem to sort out, and it must be done as soon as possible."

"What I am going to say is this: That we are more than willing to fly Jim home to England. We will cover all of the costs and we would be pleased to do this. But Ron, we would also be very pleased to keep him here, in our little plot, where all the Ruane family are. We have come to love Jim like he was our granddad. But whatever you and Pam decided will be done. I must emphasise this point. Our little plot is about a quarter of a mile from the house, peaceful and never disturbed. One more thing, Ron. If you decide to let us keep him, then I would like you and Pam to bring your partners with you, and we will pay all the costs, and I must say again, if you want him back in England then again all the costs will be taken care of. Please do exactly as you and Pam would like."

"That sounds lovely, Frank. I hope Ron and Pam decide to leave him with us. He really did love Canada; at times I think he saw himself as Canadian." "Well, here goes. I don't care what the time is in England. I have got to get this off my mind. I have to know what I must do." He dialled the number with a rather shaky hand, and after the usual delay, a voice said, "Ron here. I hope this is important." "Very important, Ron, and very sad. This is Frank in Canada and I have sadly to tell you that your father has died." "Sorry, Frank, what happened? How did it happen?" "He died, Ron, sitting on Old Swifty. The horse that he had come to love so, and the horse was standing by one of his favourite scenes; acres of wheat blowing in the breeze. These things have helped us come to terms with our very sad situation. Jim had such an effect on us. I think he felt like a real Canadian. He had a great sense of humour. He called a spade a spade. His sense of humour was more than a match for my daughter. He was a great guy."

Frank then put to Ron what he had in mind very carefully. "I will do as you suggest, Frank, and ring you as soon as I can in the morning, after I have spoken to Pam. I am very sad to have lost Dad, and sorry for the position it has placed you in. Thank you so much, Frank." "My sympathy to you and all the family, Ron. Get a little more sleep if you can. Sorry I woke you, and we will await your call. Bye Ron." Beatty stood by Frank as he spoke. "You put that very nicely, Frank. Now I am going to my chair, and then to bed. Give Debbie and Richard a call, Frank, and tell them of the probable procedure."

In the morning all ears were on the phone, listening for that call, and that is it. This is something that cannot be delayed. "Hello Frank, Ron here. I have had a good talk with Pam, and eventually we came to a decision. But as I am sure you can understand it has hit Pam rather hard. As a woman she saw things a little more compassionately, and she talked of Dad's

unhappiness since Rosieta died. Pam and I would like you to do as you have suggested and give him a place in your little plot, among those Canadians who lie there, in peace and undisturbed. Even in our cemeteries in England, that is something that is not always the case."
"Thank you, Ron and Pam. We will take good care of him, and in the years to come you will always be welcome. Now the best thing to do, Ron, when you come to Toronto airport, take an internal flight to Winnipeg airport, and we will pick you up from there. Here is my mobile number, ring me if you are in trouble." "Okay, Frank. All should be okay, but it is nice to know that in a place the size of Canada, we can soon get some help."

It has all gone according to plan. Frank and Richard have Ron, Pam, Fay and Richard in his Land Rover after a suitable welcome according to the occasion, and are on that long journey home.

Chapter Twenty Eight

Journey's End.
Jim is laid to rest.

Beatty and Debbie repeat the rather subdued welcome. It was not an occasion when one could really get excited, but the Canadians saw it as a reason to celebrate the lives of these two lovely people, rather than just to mourn. They had come to love Rosieta and Jim, even though they had known them just a few years. Frank had suggested to Ron that the family come a day or so earlier, so that they might relax before what must be a very difficult day. Pam, Jean and Richard were happy in the garden, but Ron fancied a ride on Jim's friend, Swifty. "Debbie", "yes, Ron. What's on your mind?" "Well I was wondering if you would have time to give me a riding lesson." This did bring a laugh! "Have you ever been on a horse, Ron?" "No, Debbie. I have not." Another laugh all round. "I think I could spare an hour or two. Can you hold the fort, Beatty?" "Yes. Go and give Ron a little relaxing. I think he might need it."

Debbie heaves Ron up on Old Swifty, and as she does she thinks of old Jim, and her eyes water a little. "Ready, Ron?" "Yes" he says, and gives Old Swift a gentle kick

in the ribs and the magic words, "Come on Swifty."
"How did you know that, Ron?" "Well" he says, "Dad
really did love Old Swifty, and he had spoken of him
many times, and I am already beginning to see why
he loved to ride him. By teaching him to ride, Debbie,
you did so much for him. He loved this clean, fresh,
unpolluted air, the silence, the strange calls, and the
company of that beautiful Debbie; old as he have been,
he was still very much a man, still determined to
squeeze every last drop of life out of his stay on Earth.
I think his glowing description of life on the Prairie
was what made me want to try it myself, and I must say,
what he felt so strongly I now completely understand."

They plodded on, along the track, Debbie enjoying it
as much as Ron. It was just like riding with Jim. Not a
great deal of conversation, but immensely satisfying. The
expressions on Ron's face said it all. He led a rather
hectic life at home, and this wonderful silence with a
lovely lady was marvellous. They came out of the conifers and made their way along the wheat stubble, and it
was not long before Old Swifty stopped. "Why has he
stopped, Debbie?" "Because Ron, this is where Jim
always stopped, and this is where your Dad died. Jim
loved to sit here and watch those hundreds of acres of
wheat swaying with the breeze. It has been cut now,
but Jim would still have stopped, and his mind would
have come back to that wonderful scene."

"What we shall never know, Ron, is did Jim stop
the horse, or did Swifty stop, even though perhaps
Jim had died? But what we do know is that your dad
died looking out over his favourite scenes, and we
shall keep that thought tomorrow. Well Jim, sorry Ron,
I guess this has been so like riding with your Dad, and

I have enjoyed it just as much and I hope you have.
I think those relaxed expressions on your face, and
those deep intakes of air said it all. I only wish it was
a happier occasion.

When we got back to the house, they all wanted to
know how it had been, and they had a grin on their faces,
and Ron loudly said, "It was absolutely blooming
marvellous" and with a broad smile he continued,
"Thank you, Debbie, so very much. It was something
I shall always remember. I now know what Dad
experienced as he plodded along on Old Swifty. I also
now am convinced he died a happy man."

It is the evening before the funeral and after one of
Beatty's lovely meals, they are chatting about Jim's life,
and things in general, and Frank asks the family from
England, "Have you ever thought about living in
Canada? There is lots of work here. This is a fast-
growing country." Pam's Richard was sitting opposite
Frank and he said, "Now take you, Richard. You look
like you have a bit of muscle and fifty miles up the road
there is a large lumber camp, where you work like hell,
but you get shed-load of dollars. Now what about
you, Pam? You should have a very good knowledge of
real English. You would fit in fine. And you, Ron and
Jean. Toronto would love you, and if you were not
happy there, well New York is just across the river. Well
there is something to keep you awake, but I am going
to my bed. Tomorrow I think will take a great deal
out of all of us" and with a reassuring smile, he said,
"Good night, all."

What Frank had said did make the family think, and
morning came all too soon. It was the day to say goodbye to a well-loved father, and a very good friend.

Frank's friend, Pastor John Everite, took the service. They had walked to that very peaceful place, where the Ruane family went when their time was up, and it did contrast with the destruction that occurs in some British cemeteries. Pastor John said some lovely things about Jim; that he had been given by the family, and as he spoke he said, "I would have liked to have known Jim a little more. He sounds like a man that we are so short of on Earth."

The service over, the family returned to the house, but Debbie and her Richard are still by the grave. "Richard", "yes, Debbie". "I have this very strange feeling that Rosieta is here too, and I can't seem to shake it off. Am I going crazy? It's almost unreal." "No no no, Debbie", and he wraps his arm around her. They are just the heartfelt thoughts of somebody who really loved them. Bon voyage, Jim and Rosie. Bon voyage.

Lightning Source UK Ltd.
Milton Keynes UK
UKOW04f0034171015

260701UK00001B/3/P